HOTEL TRANSYLVANIA

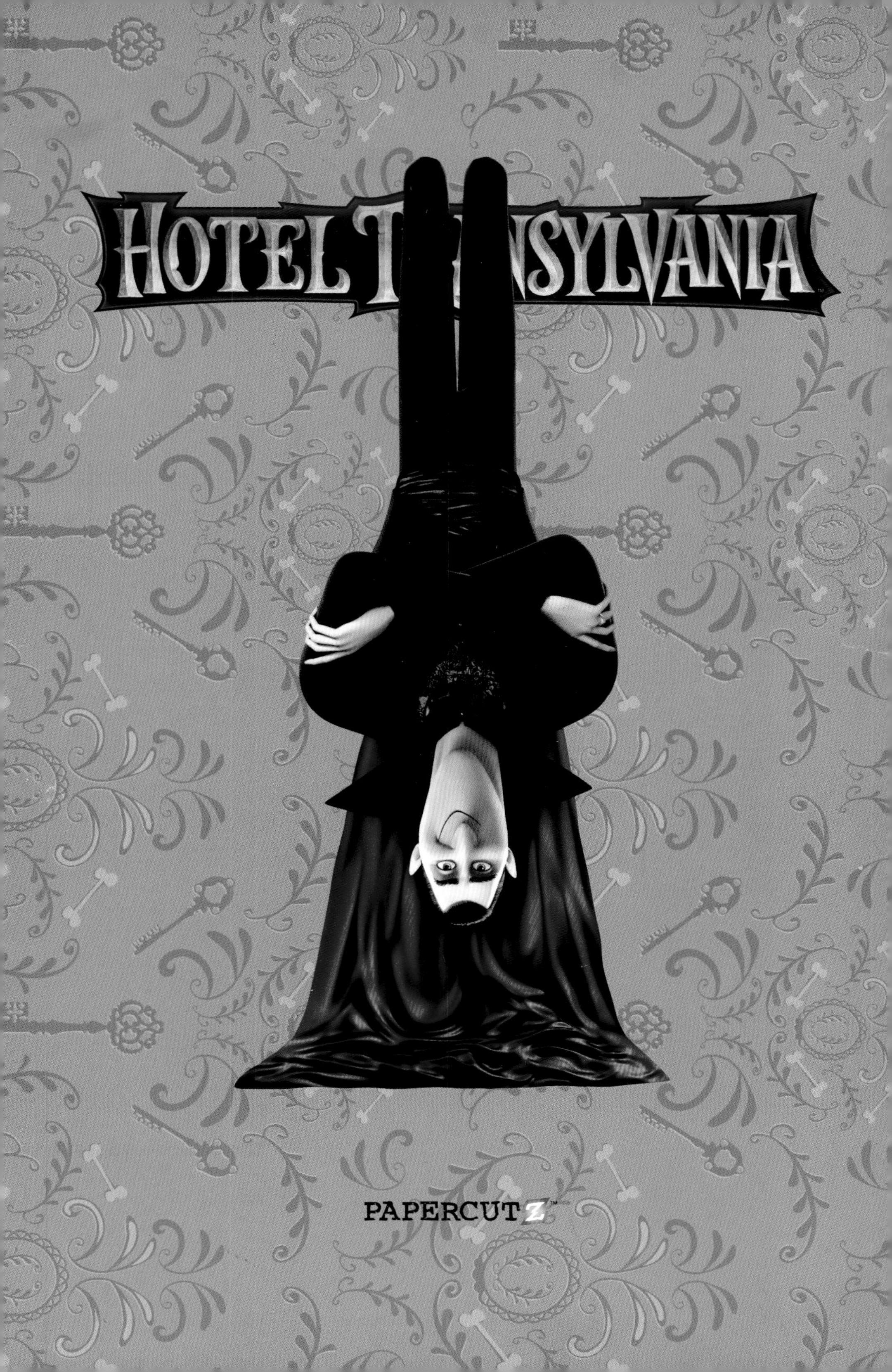

PAPERCUTZ

MORE GREAT GRAPHIC NOVEL SERIES AVAILABLE FROM PAPERCUT

THE SMURFS #21   THE GARFIELD SHOW #6   BARBIE #1   THE SISTERS #1   TROLLS #1

GERONIMO STILTON #17   THEA STILTON #6   SEA CREATURES #1   MANOSAURS #1   SCARLETT

ANNE OF GREEN BAGELS #1   DRACULA MARRIES FRANKENSTEIN!   THE RED SHOES   THE LITTLE MERMAID   FUZZY BASEBALL

HOTEL TRANSYLVANIA #1   HOTEL TRANSYLVANIA #2   THE LOUD HOUSE #1   THE ONLY LIVING BOY #5   GUMBY #1

THE SMURFS, THE GARFIELD SHOW, BARBIE, HOTEL TRANSYLVANIA, MANOSAURS, THE LOUD HOUSE and TROLLS graphic novels are available for $7.99 in paperback, and $12.99 in hardcover. THE ONLY LIVING BOY and GUMBY graphic novels are available for $8.99 in paperback, and $13.9 hardcover. GERONIMO STILTON and THEA STILTON graphic novels are available for $9.99 in hardcover only. FUZZY BASEBALL graphic novels are avai for $9.99 in paperback only. THE LUNCH WITCH, SCARLETT, and ANNE OF GREEN BAGELS graphic novels are available for $14.99 in paperback c THE RED SHOES and THE LITTLE MERMAID graphic novels are available for $12.99 in hardcover only. DRACULA MARRIES FRANKENSTEIN! graphic nove available for $12.99 in paperback only. THE SISTERS graphic novels are available for $9.99 in paperback, and $14.99 in hardcover. SEA CREATURES g novels are available for $10.99 in hardcover only.

Available from booksellers everywhere. You can also order online from www.papercutz.com. Or call 1-800-886-1223, Monday through Friday, 9–5 EST. Visa, and AmEx accepted. To order by mail, please add $5.00 for postage and handling for first book ordered, $1.00 for each additional book and mo check payable to NBM Publishing. Send to: Papercutz, 160 Broadway, Suite 700, East Wing, New York, NY 10038.

THE SMURFS, GUMBY, THE GARFIELD SHOW, THE LOUD HOUSE, THE ONLY LIVING BOY, BARBIE, TROLLS, GERONIMO STILTON, THEA STILTON, FU BASEBALL, THE LUNCH WITCH, THE LITTLE MERMAID, HOTEL TRANSYLVANIA, MANOSAURS, THE SISTERS, SEA CREATURES ,THE RED SHOES, ANN GREEN BAGELS, DRACULA MARRIES FRANKENSTEIN!, and SCARLETT graphic novels are also available wherever e-books are sold.

HOTEL TRANSYLVANIA

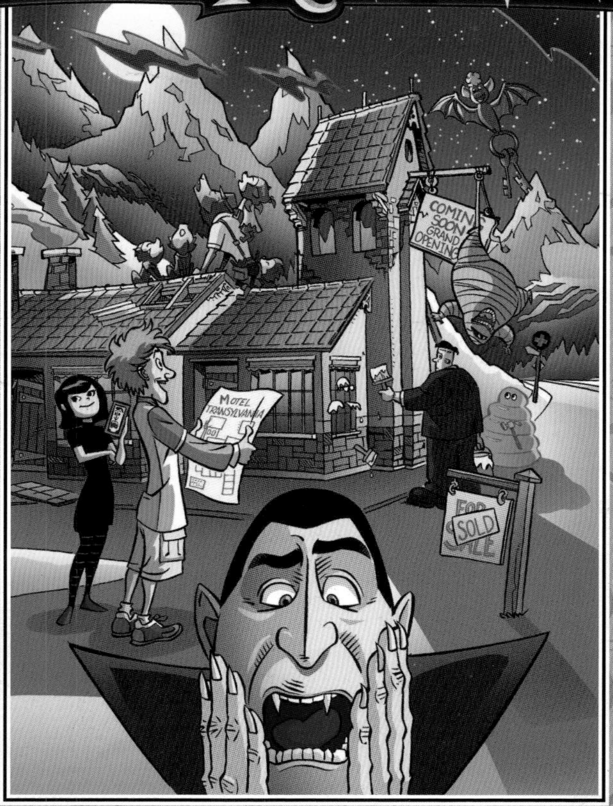
COMIN
SOON
GRAND
OPENING
MOTEL
TRANSYLVANIA
SOLD

MOTEL TRANSYLVANIA

STEFAN PETRUCHA–WRITER
ALLEN GLADFELTER
& ZAZO–ARTISTS

PAPERCUTZ
NEW YORK

#3 "Motel Transylvania"
STEFAN PETRUCHA—Writer
ALLEN GLADFELTER—Penciler
ZAZO—Inker
LAURIE E. SMITH—Colorist
WILSON RAMOS JR.—Letterer
DAWN GUZZO—Production
JEFF WHITMAN—Assistant Managing Editor
JIM SALICRUP
Editor-in-Chief

Special thanks to Keith Baxter, Melissa Sturm, Virginia King, Rick Mischel, PH Marcondes, and everyone at Sony Pictures Animation

ISBN: 978-1-54580-015-7

Papercutz books may be purchased for business or promotional use.
For information on bulk purchases please contact Macmillan Corporate
and Premium Sales Department at (800) 221-795 x5442.

Printed in China
June 2018

Distributed by Macmillan
First Printing

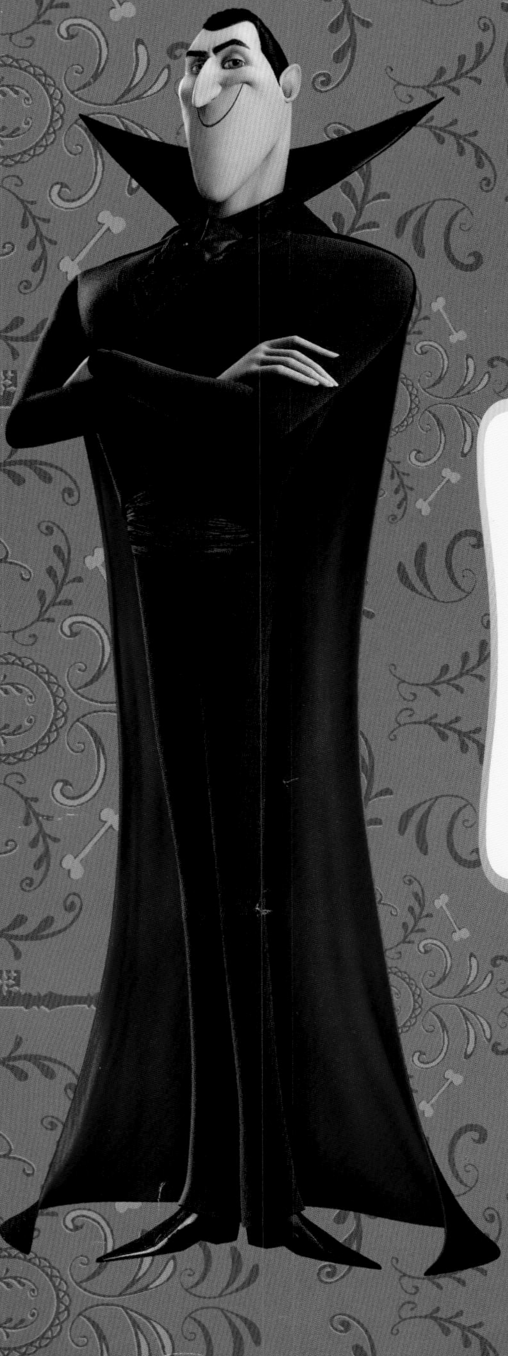

DRAC

Legendary monster and Hotelier extraordinaire, Drac is finally enjoying the perks of his monster and human filled Hotel Transylvania — as well as being a loving father and grandfather! Running your own business can be a huge pain in the neck but luckily he's got the trusty Drac Pack by his side as well as his loyal and ever-loving daughter Mavis.

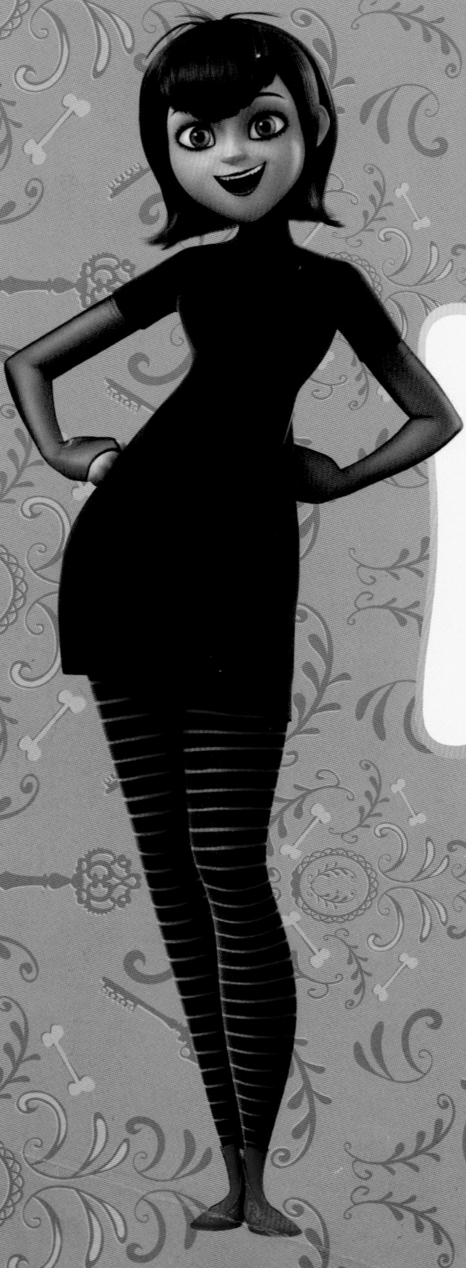

MAVIS

Daughter, wife, mom, and now assistant Hotel Transylvania manager, Mavis does it all! She's curious, optimistic and deeply loyal to her monster and human family. She is also a strong, courageous, independent, young vampire, but in the end she will always be Daddy's little bat.

JOHNNY

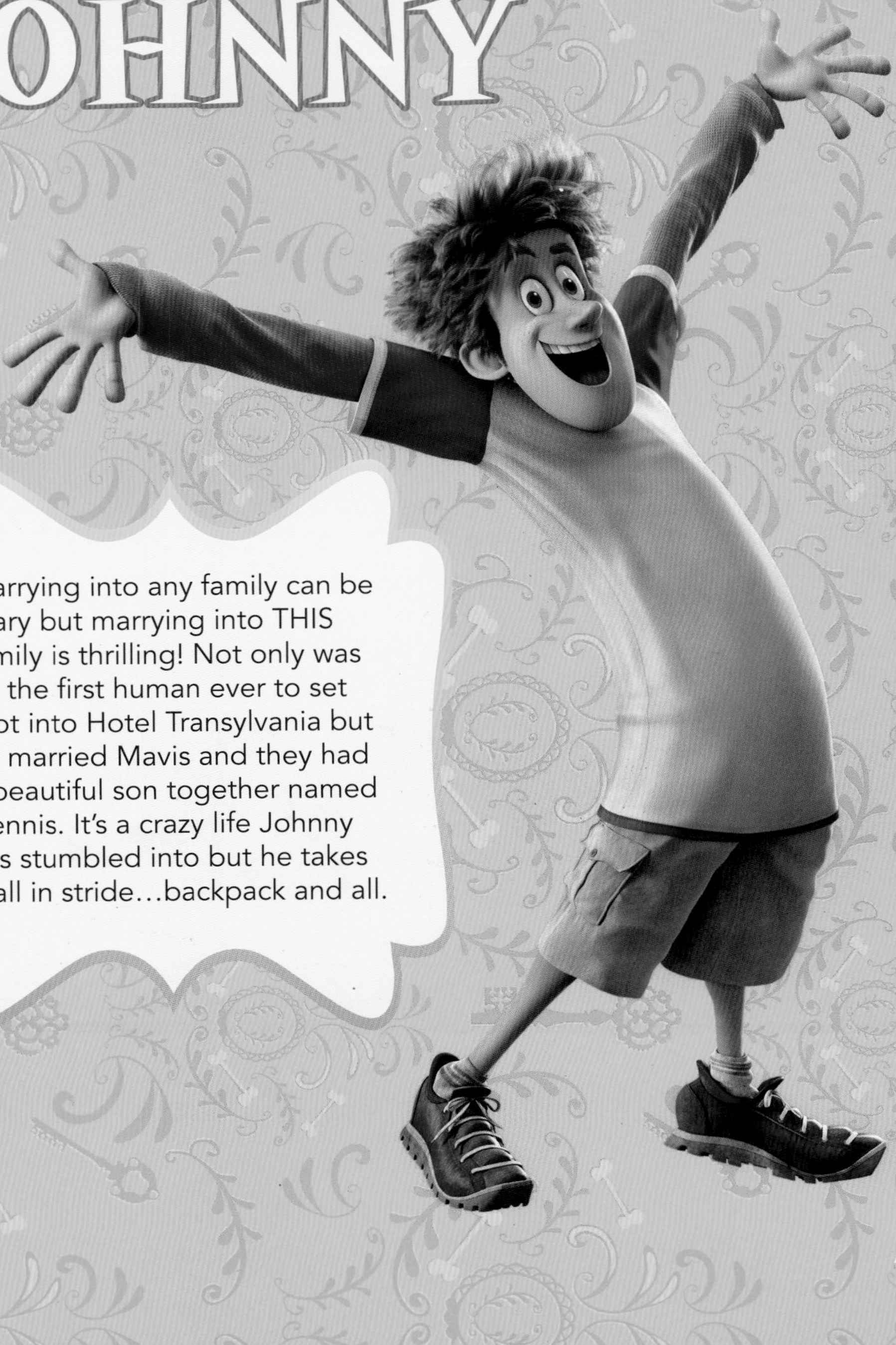

Marrying into any family can be scary but marrying into THIS family is thrilling! Not only was he the first human ever to set foot into Hotel Transylvania but he married Mavis and they had a beautiful son together named Dennis. It's a crazy life Johnny has stumbled into but he takes it all in stride...backpack and all.

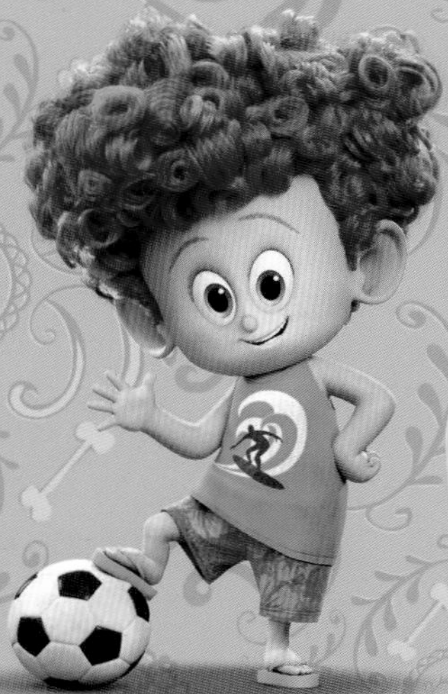

DENNIS

All vampires have until their fifth birthday to sprout their fangs…and wouldn't you know it…Mavis and Johnny's son did! Dennis is a curly-haired, curious kid, who just wants to sneak off and have adventures with his best wolf pup friend, Winnie, and new pup, Tinkles.

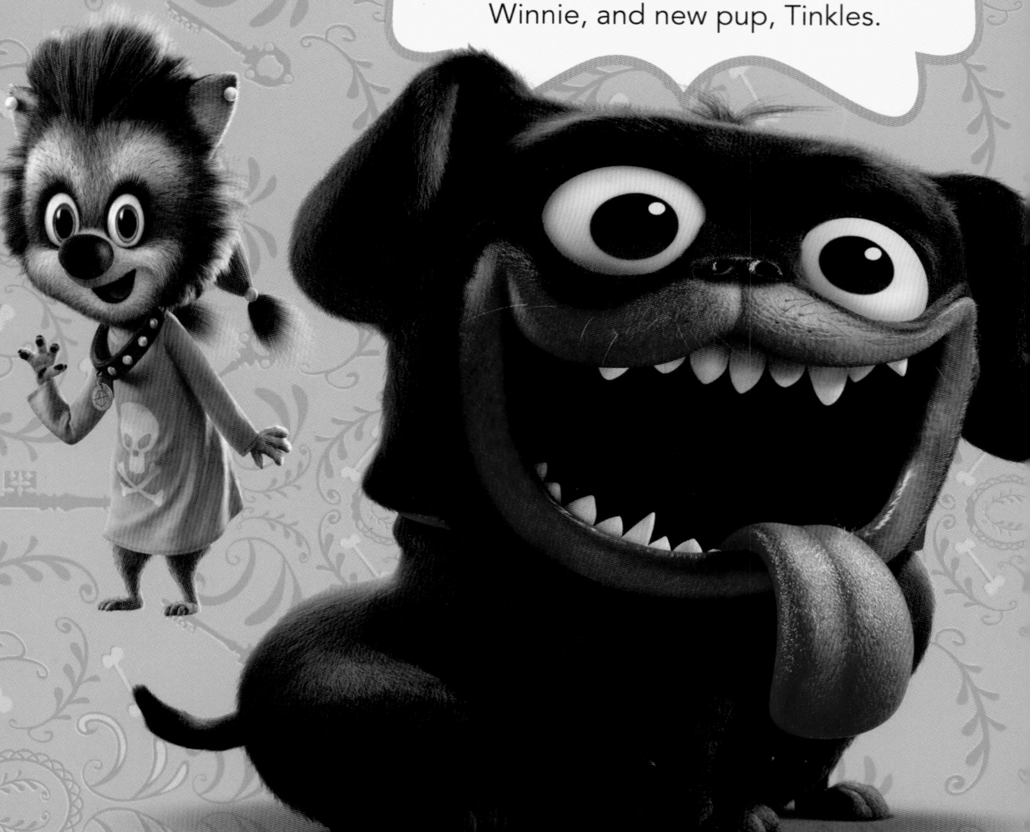

FRANK

Frank is a guy who will always leave you in stitches! He's one of Drac's best friends and is always there to lend a hand, an arm, or a leg.

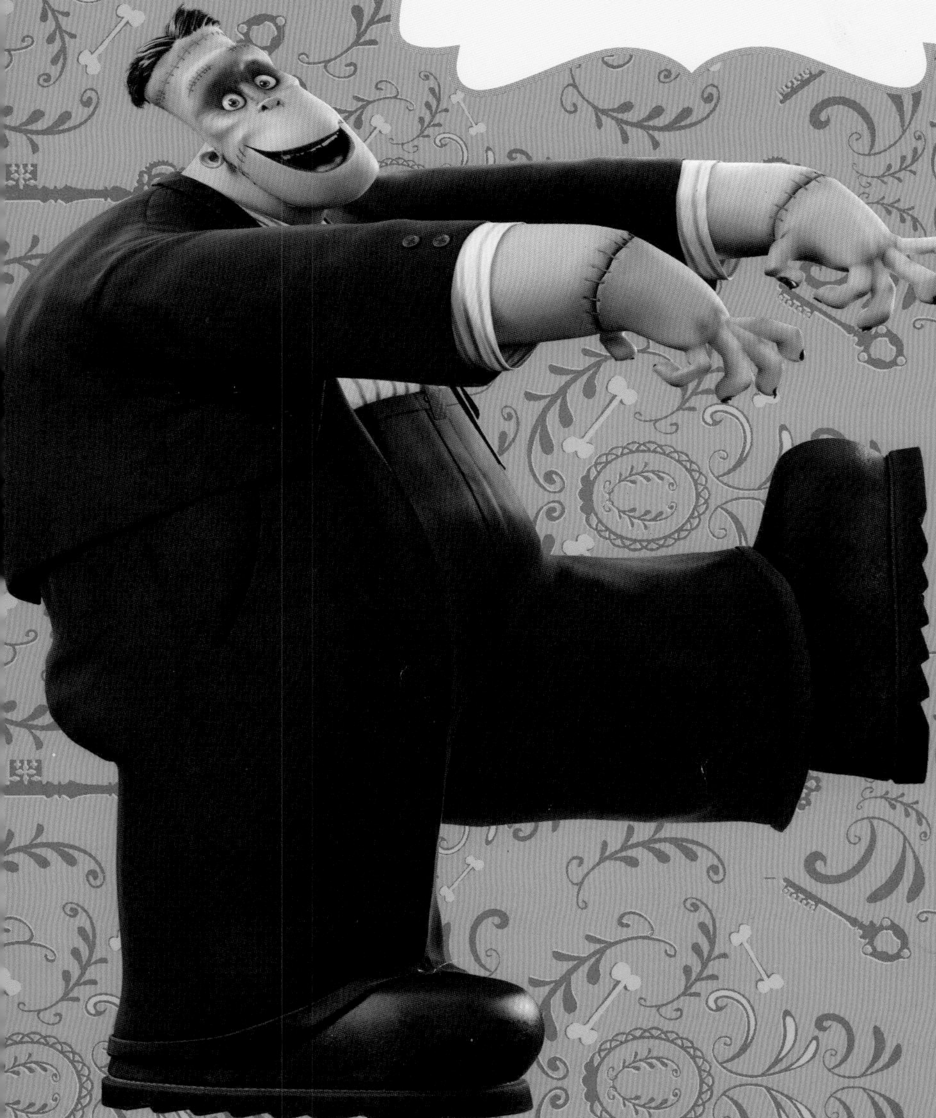

MURRAY

Murray, the mummy, is the life of the party and is always there to bandage any problem Drac may have.

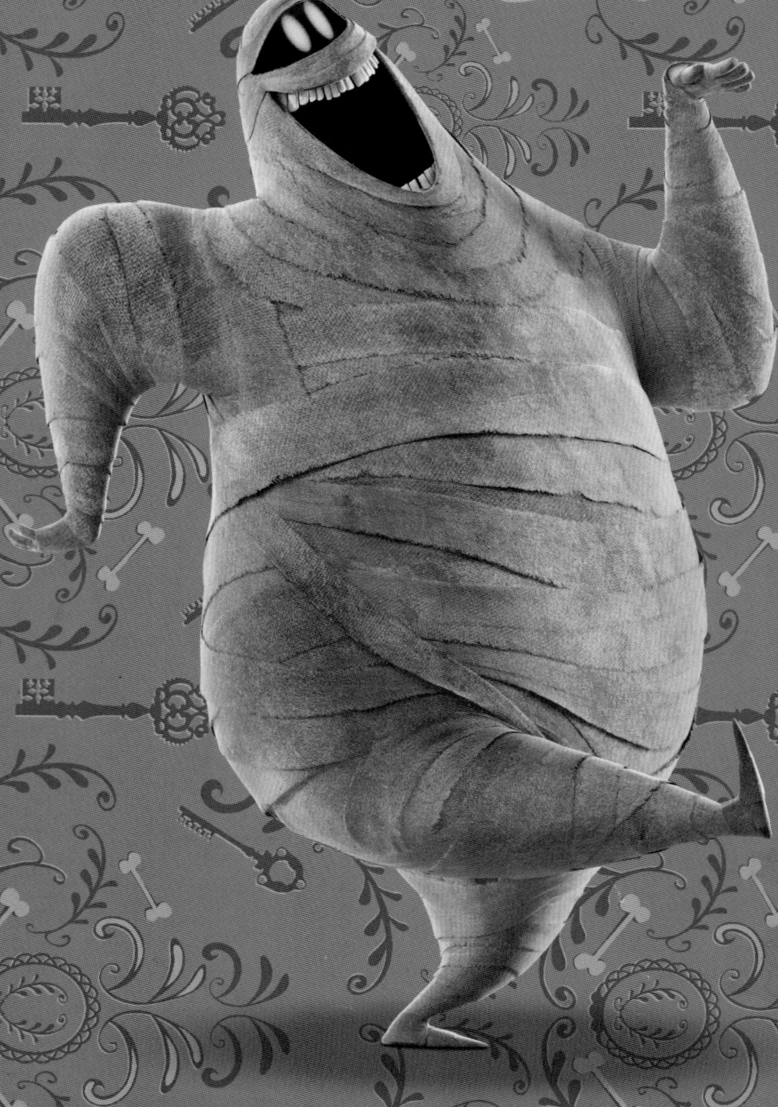

WAYNE

Wayne, the werewolf, would love to be howling at the moon but he has no time! He's got a gazillion wolf pups along with his wife Wanda to take care of. In his little free time, Wayne enjoys teaching tennis and playing fetch — at the same time! — as well as rocking the bass.

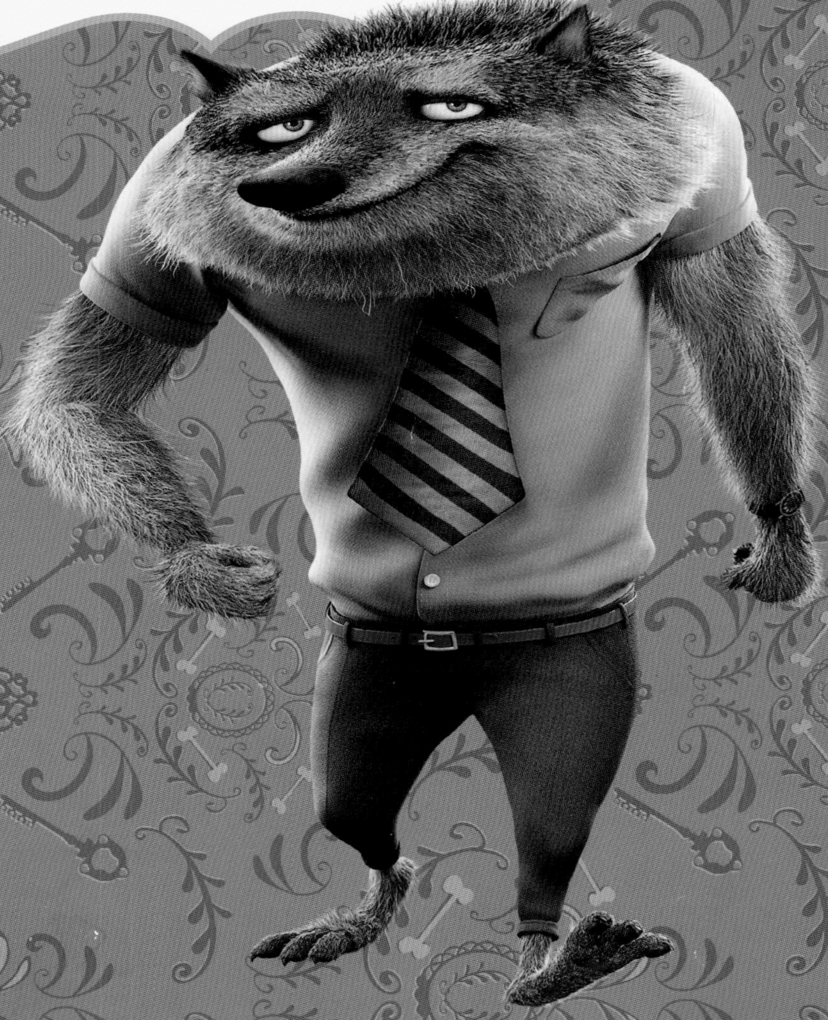

GRIFFIN

The infamous Invisible Man has a frustrating habit of sneaking up on his friends. Make sure you check out his best-selling exercise videos, just be warned, they're a bit hard to follow!

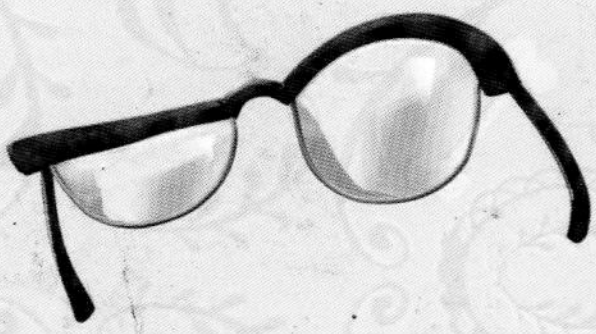

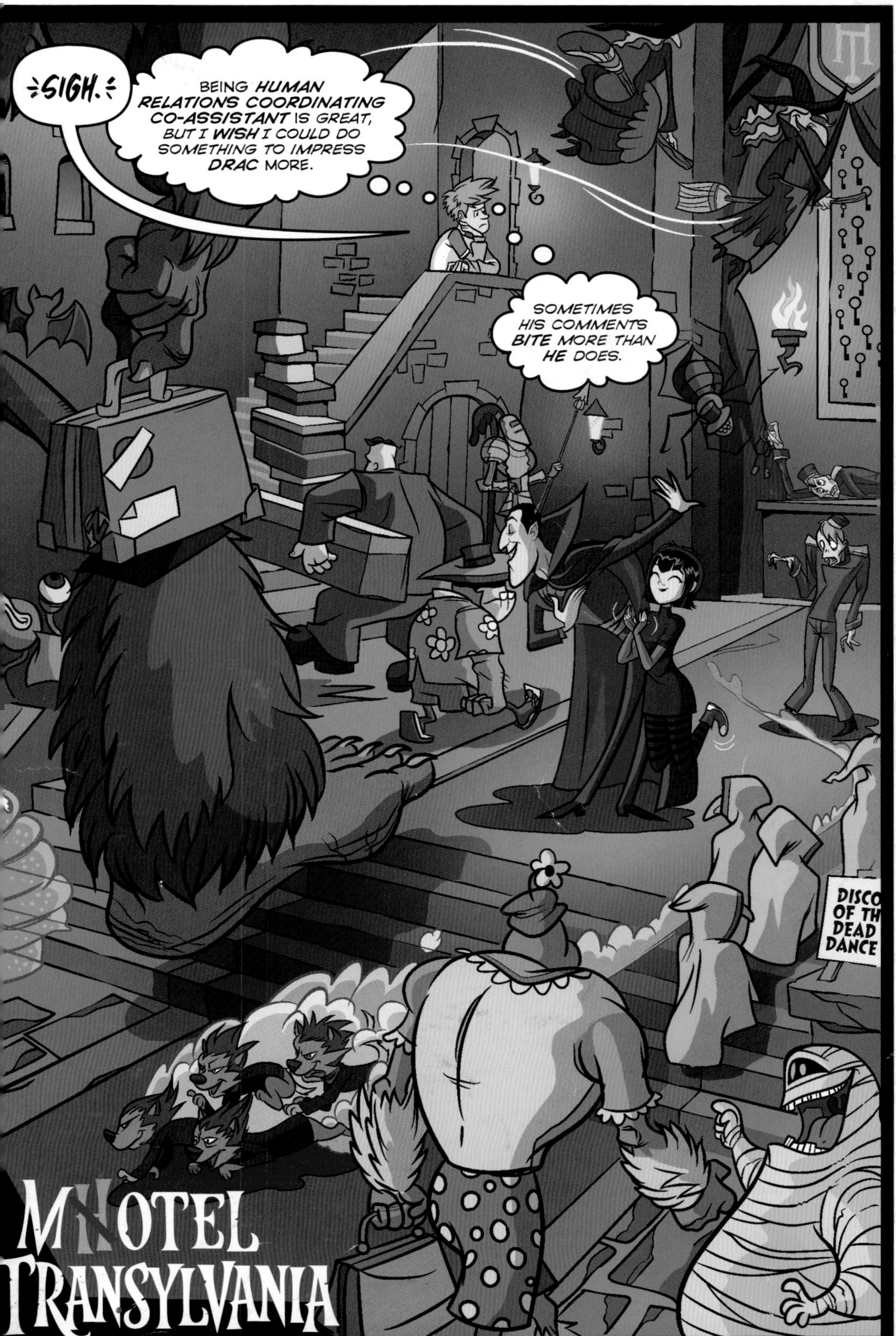
SIGH.
BEING HUMAN RELATIONS COORDINATING CO-ASSISTANT IS GREAT, BUT I WISH I COULD DO SOMETHING TO IMPRESS DRAC MORE.
SOMETIMES HIS COMMENTS BITE MORE THAN HE DOES.
DISCO OF TH DEAD DANCE
MHOTEL TRANSYLVANIA

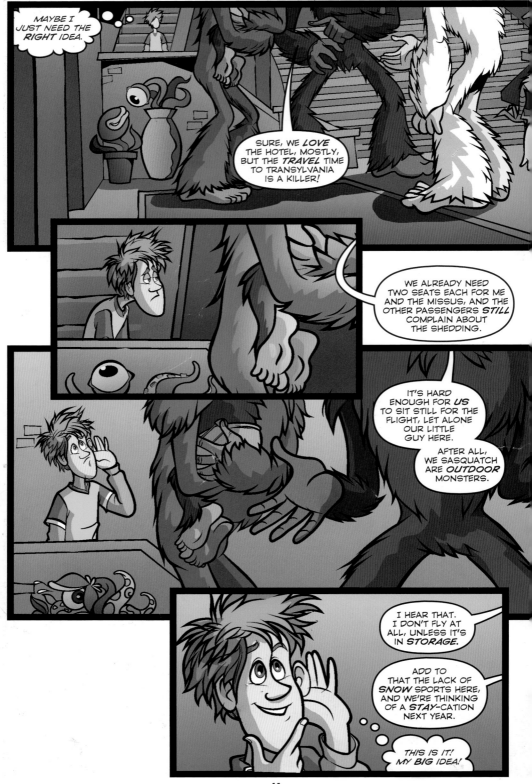

MAYBE I JUST NEED THE *RIGHT* IDEA.

SURE, WE *LOVE* THE HOTEL, MOSTLY, BUT THE *TRAVEL* TIME TO TRANSYLVANIA IS A KILLER!

WE ALREADY NEED TWO SEATS EACH FOR ME AND THE MISSUS, AND THE OTHER PASSENGERS *STILL* COMPLAIN ABOUT THE SHEDDING.

IT'S HARD ENOUGH FOR *US* TO SIT STILL FOR THE FLIGHT, LET ALONE OUR LITTLE GUY HERE.

AFTER ALL, WE SASQUATCH ARE *OUTDOOR* MONSTERS.

I HEAR THAT. I DON'T FLY AT ALL, UNLESS IT'S IN *STORAGE*.

ADD TO THAT THE LACK OF *SNOW* SPORTS HERE, AND WE'RE THINKING OF A *STAY*-CATION NEXT YEAR.

THIS IS IT! MY *BIG* IDEA!

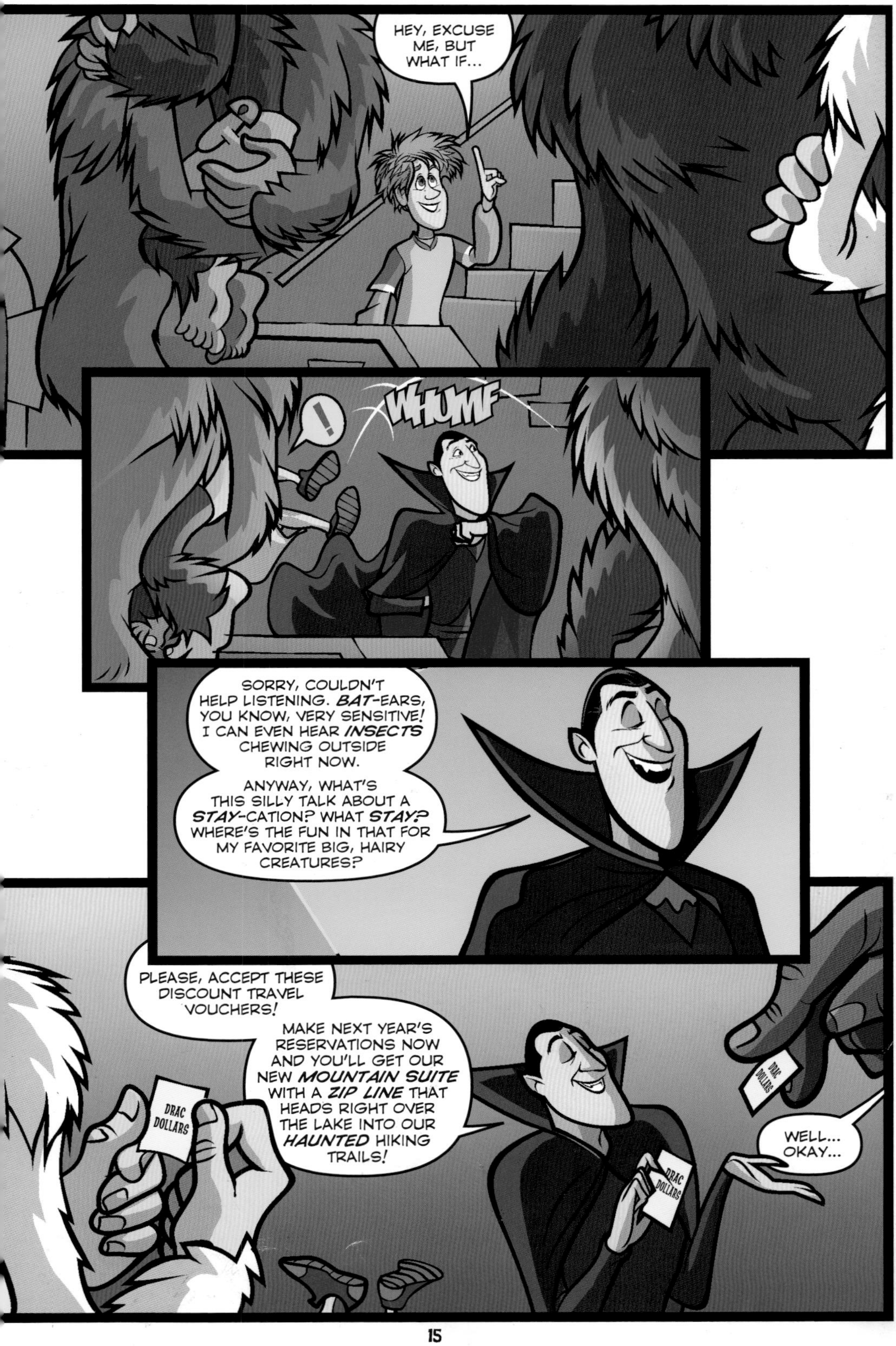
HEY, EXCUSE ME, BUT WHAT IF...
!
WHUMF
SORRY, COULDN'T HELP LISTENING. BAT-EARS, YOU KNOW, VERY SENSITIVE! I CAN EVEN HEAR INSECTS CHEWING OUTSIDE RIGHT NOW.
ANYWAY, WHAT'S THIS SILLY TALK ABOUT A STAY-CATION? WHAT STAY? WHERE'S THE FUN IN THAT FOR MY FAVORITE BIG, HAIRY CREATURES?
PLEASE, ACCEPT THESE DISCOUNT TRAVEL VOUCHERS!
MAKE NEXT YEAR'S RESERVATIONS NOW AND YOU'LL GET OUR NEW MOUNTAIN SUITE WITH A ZIP LINE THAT HEADS RIGHT OVER THE LAKE INTO OUR HAUNTED HIKING TRAILS!
DRAC DOLLARS
DRAC DOLLARS
DRAC DOLLARS
WELL... OKAY...

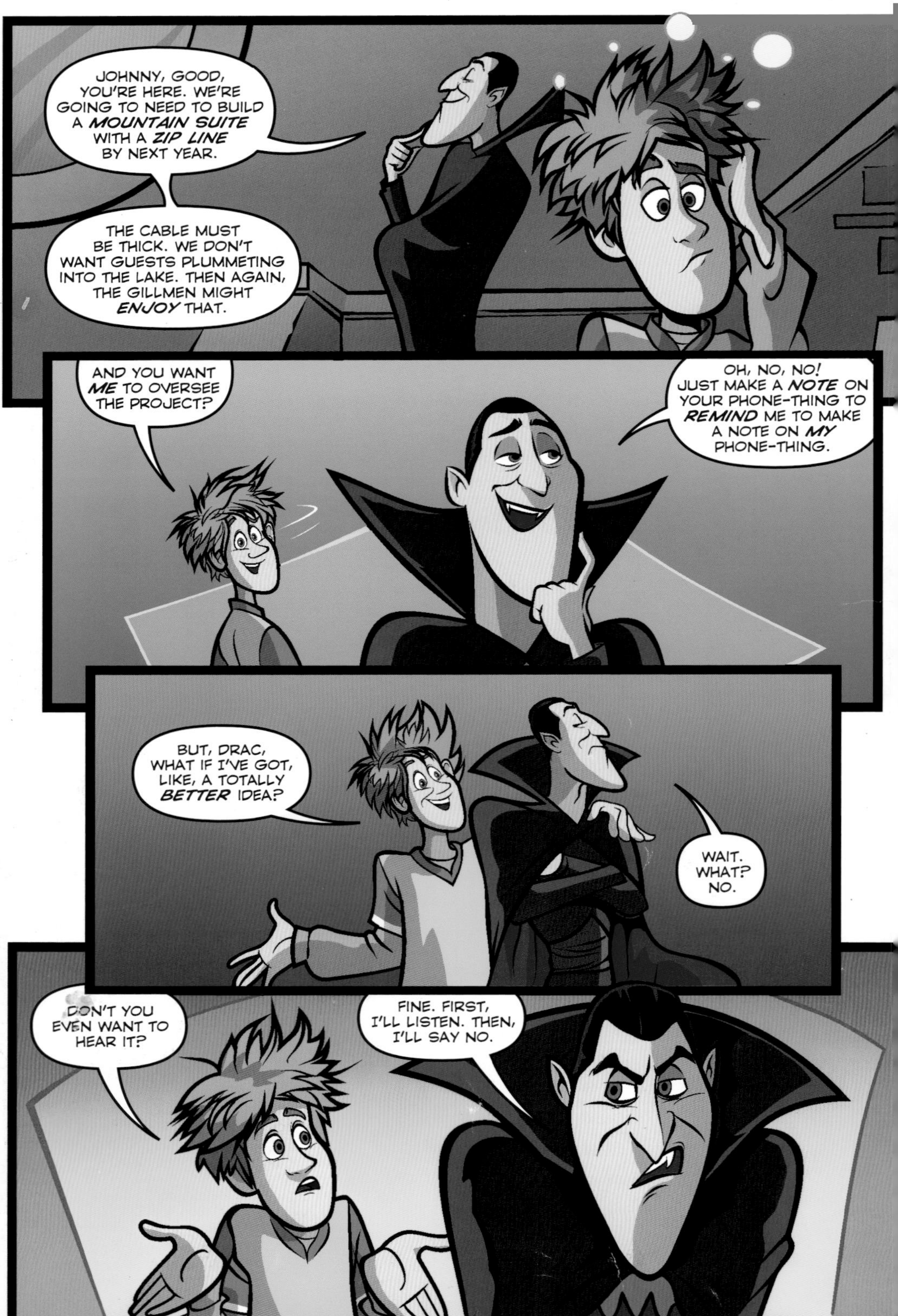
JOHNNY, GOOD, YOU'RE HERE. WE'RE GOING TO NEED TO BUILD A *MOUNTAIN SUITE* WITH A *ZIP LINE* BY NEXT YEAR.
THE CABLE MUST BE THICK. WE DON'T WANT GUESTS PLUMMETING INTO THE LAKE. THEN AGAIN, THE GILLMEN MIGHT *ENJOY* THAT.
AND YOU WANT *ME* TO OVERSEE THE PROJECT?
OH, NO, NO! JUST MAKE A *NOTE* ON YOUR PHONE-THING TO *REMIND* ME TO MAKE A NOTE ON *MY* PHONE-THING.
BUT, DRAC, WHAT IF I'VE GOT, LIKE, A TOTALLY *BETTER* IDEA?
WAIT. WHAT? NO.
DON'T YOU EVEN WANT TO HEAR IT?
FINE. FIRST, I'LL LISTEN. THEN, I'LL SAY NO.

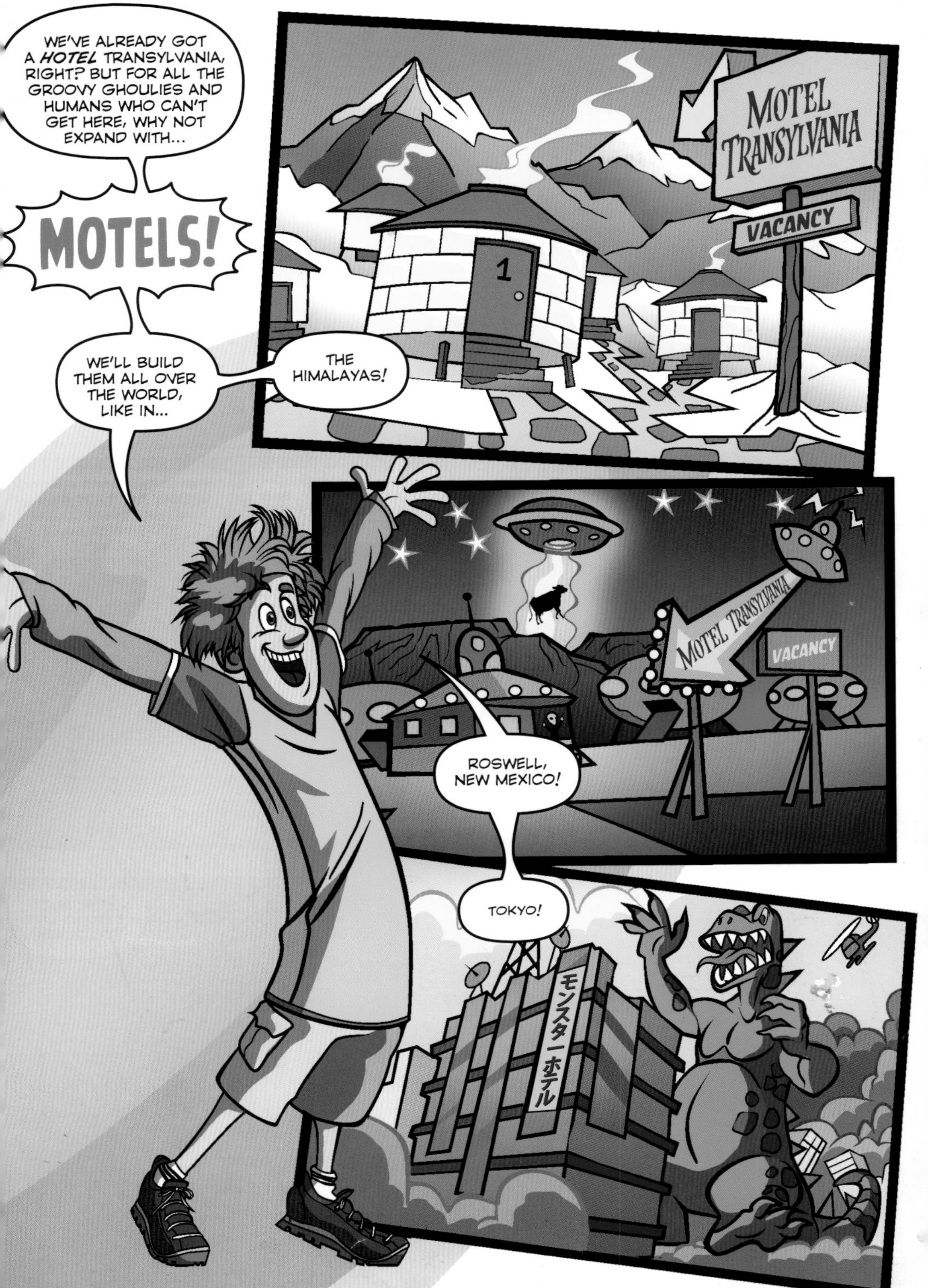
WE'VE ALREADY GOT A HOTEL TRANSYLVANIA, RIGHT? BUT FOR ALL THE GROOVY GHOULIES AND HUMANS WHO CAN'T GET HERE, WHY NOT EXPAND WITH...
MOTELS!
WE'LL BUILD THEM ALL OVER THE WORLD, LIKE IN...
THE HIMALAYAS!
MOTEL TRANSYLVANIA
VACANCY
1
ROSWELL, NEW MEXICO!
MOTEL TRANSYLVANIA
VACANCY
TOKYO!
モンスターホテル

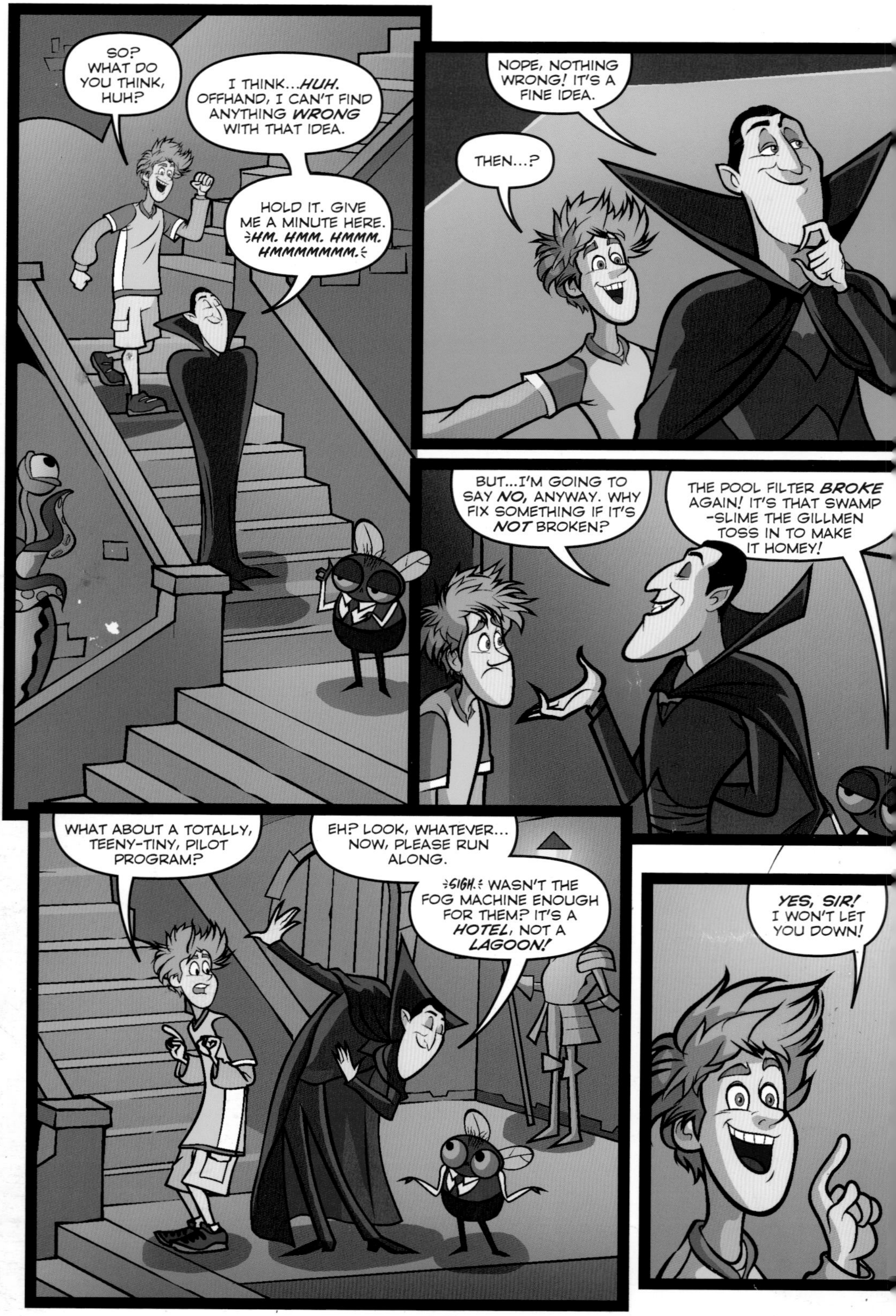
SO? WHAT DO YOU THINK, HUH?
I THINK...HUH. OFFHAND, I CAN'T FIND ANYTHING WRONG WITH THAT IDEA.
HOLD IT. GIVE ME A MINUTE HERE. HM. HMM. HMMM. HMMMMMMM.
NOPE, NOTHING WRONG! IT'S A FINE IDEA.
THEN...?
BUT...I'M GOING TO SAY NO, ANYWAY. WHY FIX SOMETHING IF IT'S NOT BROKEN?
THE POOL FILTER BROKE AGAIN! IT'S THAT SWAMP-SLIME THE GILLMEN TOSS IN TO MAKE IT HOMEY!
WHAT ABOUT A TOTALLY, TEENY-TINY, PILOT PROGRAM?
EH? LOOK, WHATEVER... NOW, PLEASE RUN ALONG.
SIGH. WASN'T THE FOG MACHINE ENOUGH FOR THEM? IT'S A HOTEL, NOT A LAGOON!
YES, SIR! I WON'T LET YOU DOWN!

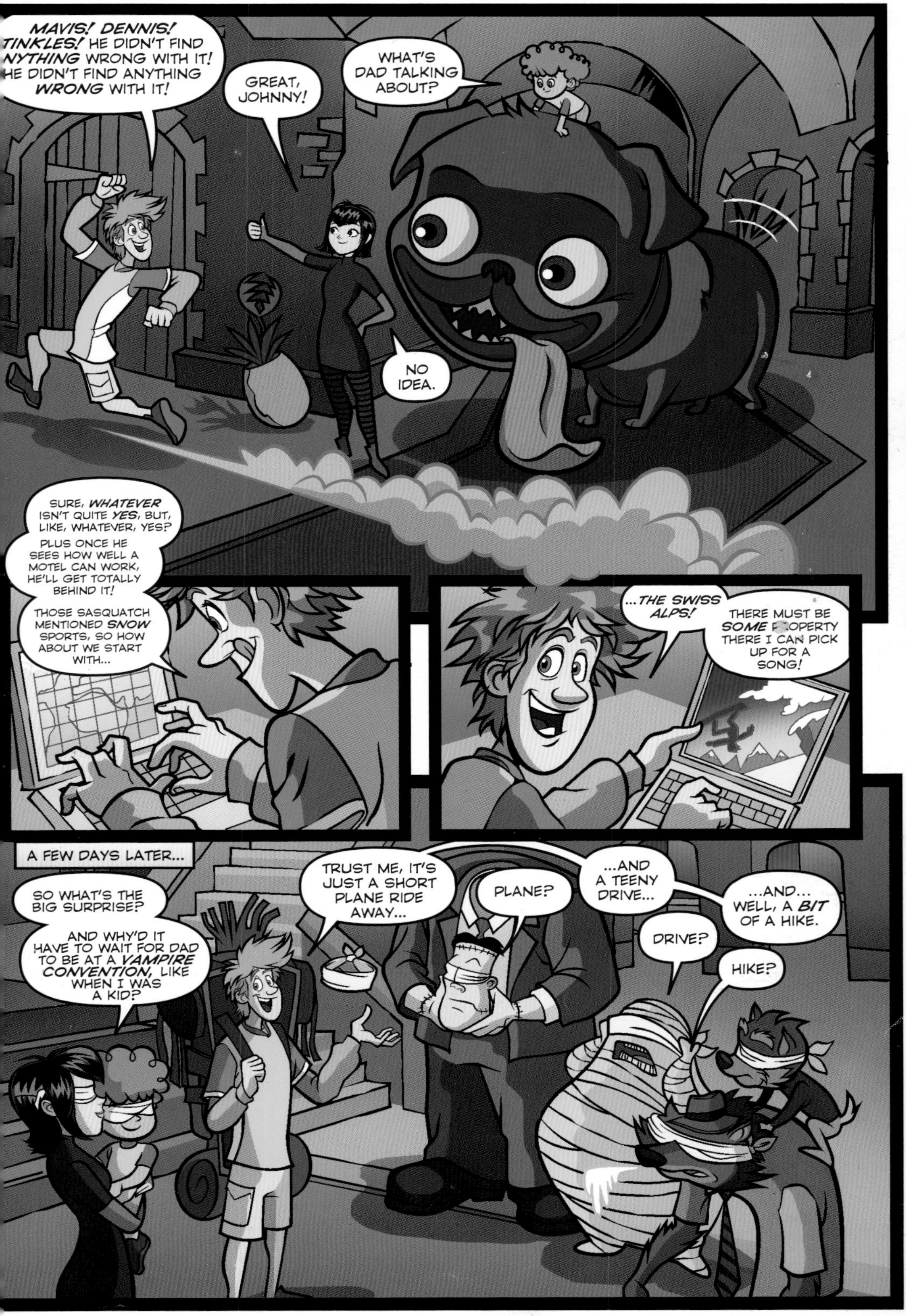
MAVIS! DENNIS! TINKLES! HE DIDN'T FIND NYTHING WRONG WITH IT! HE DIDN'T FIND ANYTHING WRONG WITH IT!
GREAT, JOHNNY!
WHAT'S DAD TALKING ABOUT?
NO IDEA.
SURE, WHATEVER ISN'T QUITE YES, BUT, LIKE, WHATEVER, YES?
PLUS ONCE HE SEES HOW WELL A MOTEL CAN WORK, HE'LL GET TOTALLY BEHIND IT!
THOSE SASQUATCH MENTIONED SNOW SPORTS, SO HOW ABOUT WE START WITH...
...THE SWISS ALPS!
THERE MUST BE SOME PROPERTY THERE I CAN PICK UP FOR A SONG!
A FEW DAYS LATER...
SO WHAT'S THE BIG SURPRISE?
AND WHY'D IT HAVE TO WAIT FOR DAD TO BE AT A VAMPIRE CONVENTION, LIKE WHEN I WAS A KID?
TRUST ME, IT'S JUST A SHORT PLANE RIDE AWAY...
PLANE?
...AND A TEENY DRIVE...
DRIVE?
...AND... WELL, A BIT OF A HIKE.
HIKE?

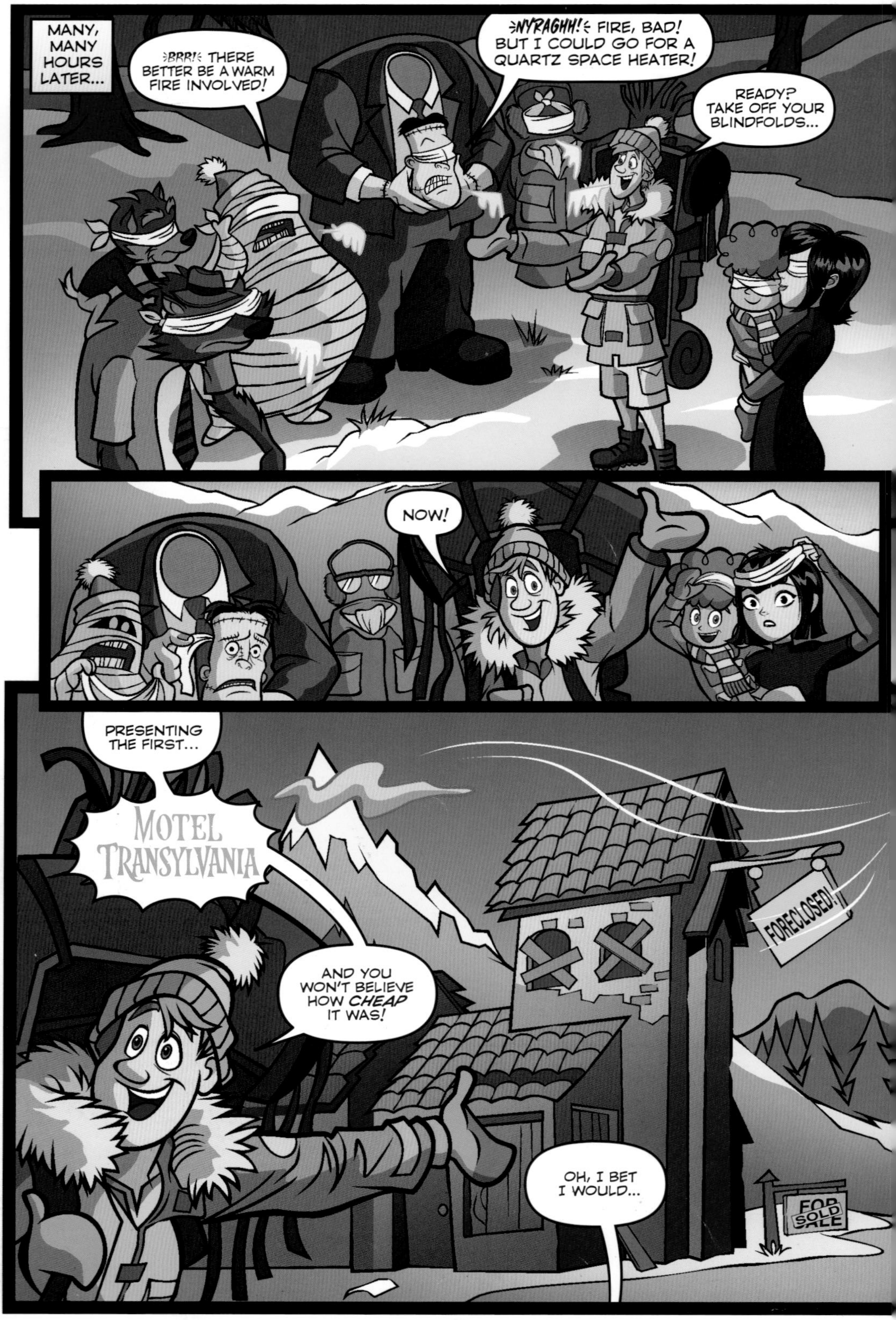
MANY, MANY HOURS LATER...
BRRR! THERE BETTER BE A WARM FIRE INVOLVED!
NYRAGHH! FIRE, BAD! BUT I COULD GO FOR A QUARTZ SPACE HEATER!
READY? TAKE OFF YOUR BLINDFOLDS...
NOW!
PRESENTING THE FIRST...
MOTEL TRANSYLVANIA
AND YOU WON'T BELIEVE HOW CHEAP IT WAS!
FORECLOSED!
OH, I BET I WOULD...
FOR SALE
SOLD

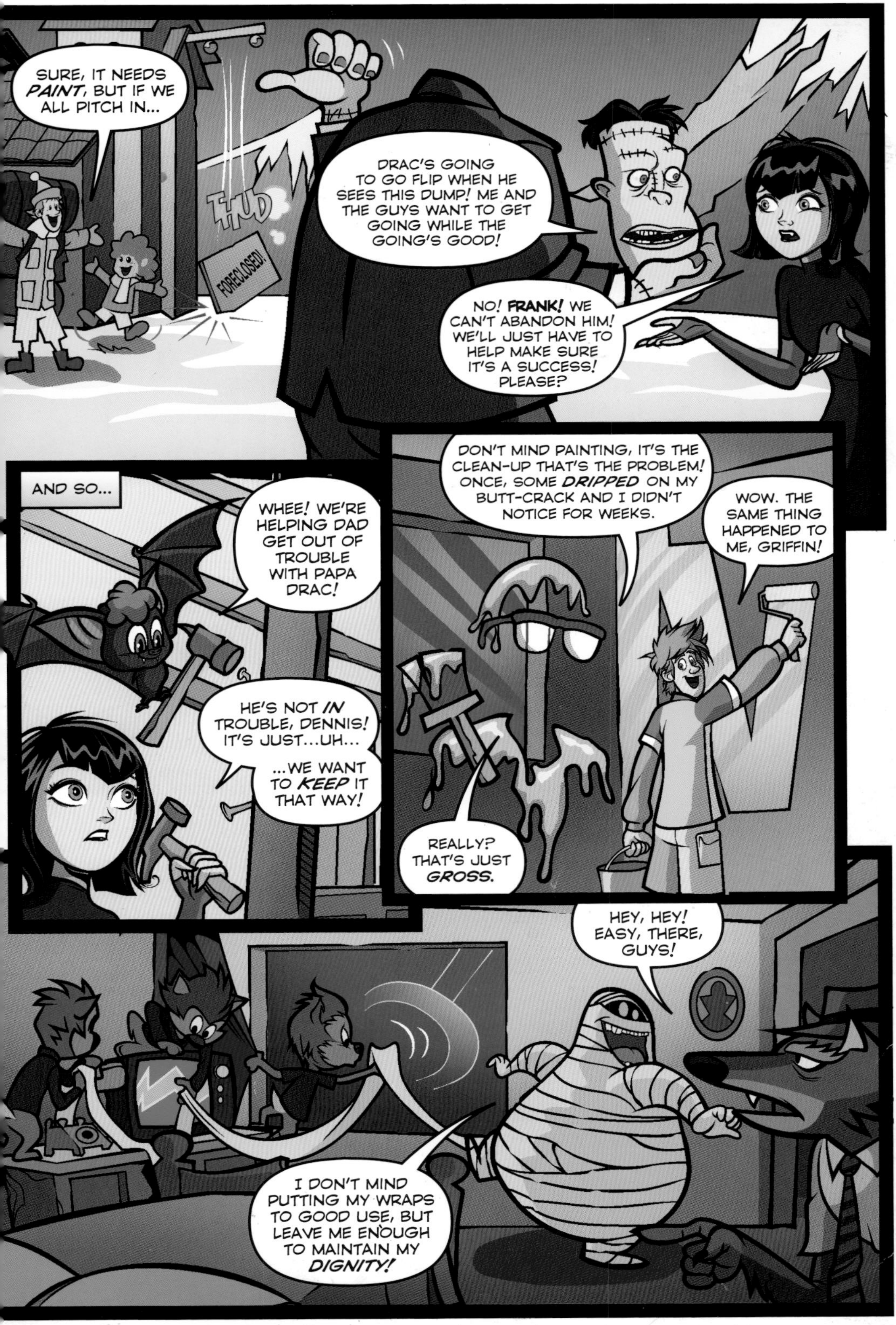
SURE, IT NEEDS PAINT, BUT IF WE ALL PITCH IN...
THUD
FORECLOSED!
DRAC'S GOING TO GO FLIP WHEN HE SEES THIS DUMP! ME AND THE GUYS WANT TO GET GOING WHILE THE GOING'S GOOD!
NO! FRANK! WE CAN'T ABANDON HIM! WE'LL JUST HAVE TO HELP MAKE SURE IT'S A SUCCESS! PLEASE?
AND SO...
WHEE! WE'RE HELPING DAD GET OUT OF TROUBLE WITH PAPA DRAC!
HE'S NOT IN TROUBLE, DENNIS! IT'S JUST...UH...
...WE WANT TO KEEP IT THAT WAY!
DON'T MIND PAINTING, IT'S THE CLEAN-UP THAT'S THE PROBLEM! ONCE, SOME DRIPPED ON MY BUTT-CRACK AND I DIDN'T NOTICE FOR WEEKS.
WOW. THE SAME THING HAPPENED TO ME, GRIFFIN!
REALLY? THAT'S JUST GROSS.
HEY, HEY! EASY, THERE, GUYS!
I DON'T MIND PUTTING MY WRAPS TO GOOD USE, BUT LEAVE ME ENOUGH TO MAINTAIN MY DIGNITY!

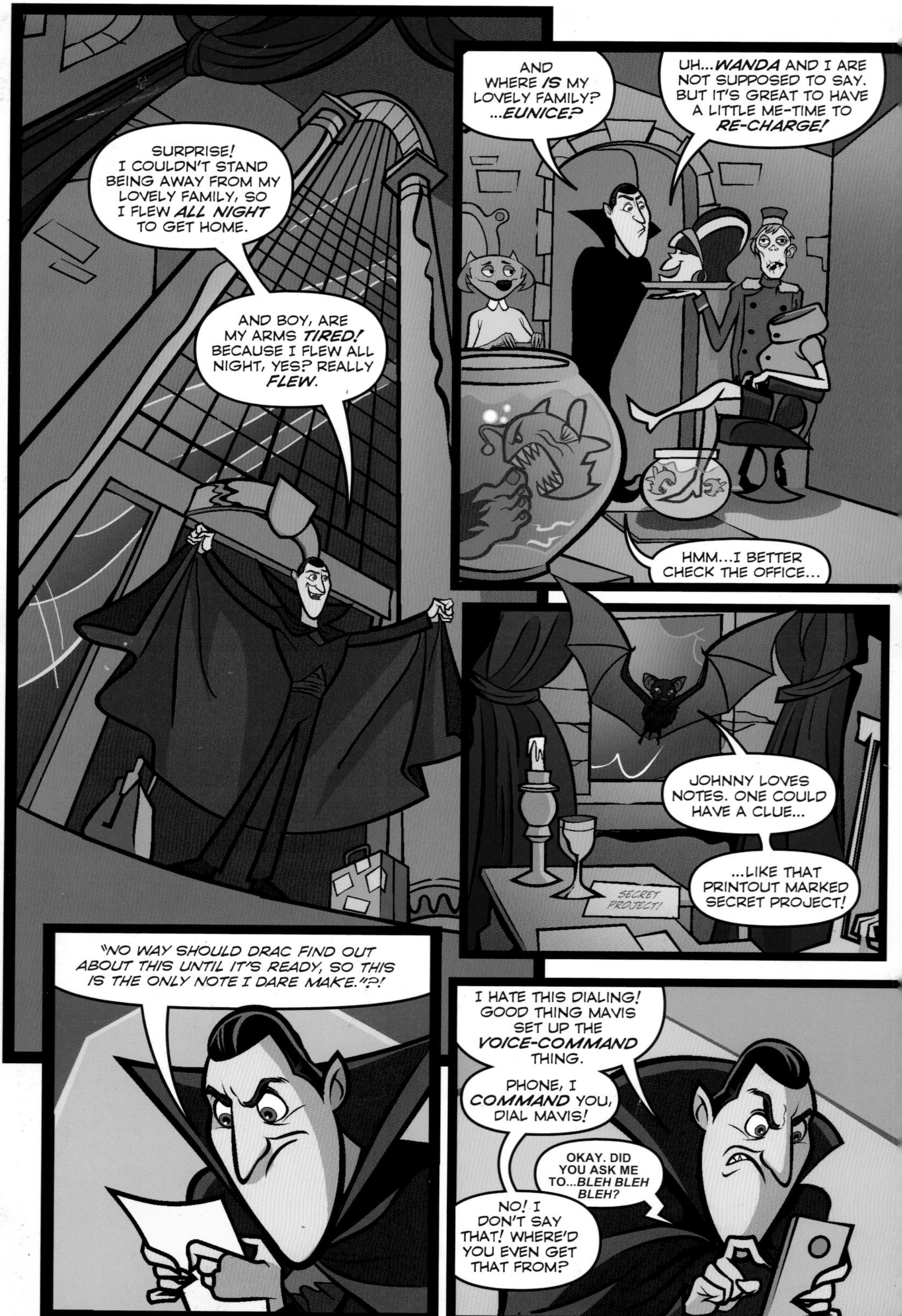
SURPRISE! I COULDN'T STAND BEING AWAY FROM MY LOVELY FAMILY, SO I FLEW ALL NIGHT TO GET HOME.
AND BOY, ARE MY ARMS TIRED! BECAUSE I FLEW ALL NIGHT, YES? REALLY FLEW.
AND WHERE IS MY LOVELY FAMILY? ...EUNICE?
UH...WANDA AND I ARE NOT SUPPOSED TO SAY. BUT IT'S GREAT TO HAVE A LITTLE ME-TIME TO RE-CHARGE!
HMM...I BETTER CHECK THE OFFICE...
JOHNNY LOVES NOTES. ONE COULD HAVE A CLUE...
...LIKE THAT PRINTOUT MARKED SECRET PROJECT!
SECRET PROJECT!
"NO WAY SHOULD DRAC FIND OUT ABOUT THIS UNTIL IT'S READY, SO THIS IS THE ONLY NOTE I DARE MAKE."?!
I HATE THIS DIALING! GOOD THING MAVIS SET UP THE VOICE-COMMAND THING.
PHONE, I COMMAND YOU, DIAL MAVIS!
OKAY. DID YOU ASK ME TO...BLEH BLEH BLEH?
NO! I DON'T SAY THAT! WHERE'D YOU EVEN GET THAT FROM?

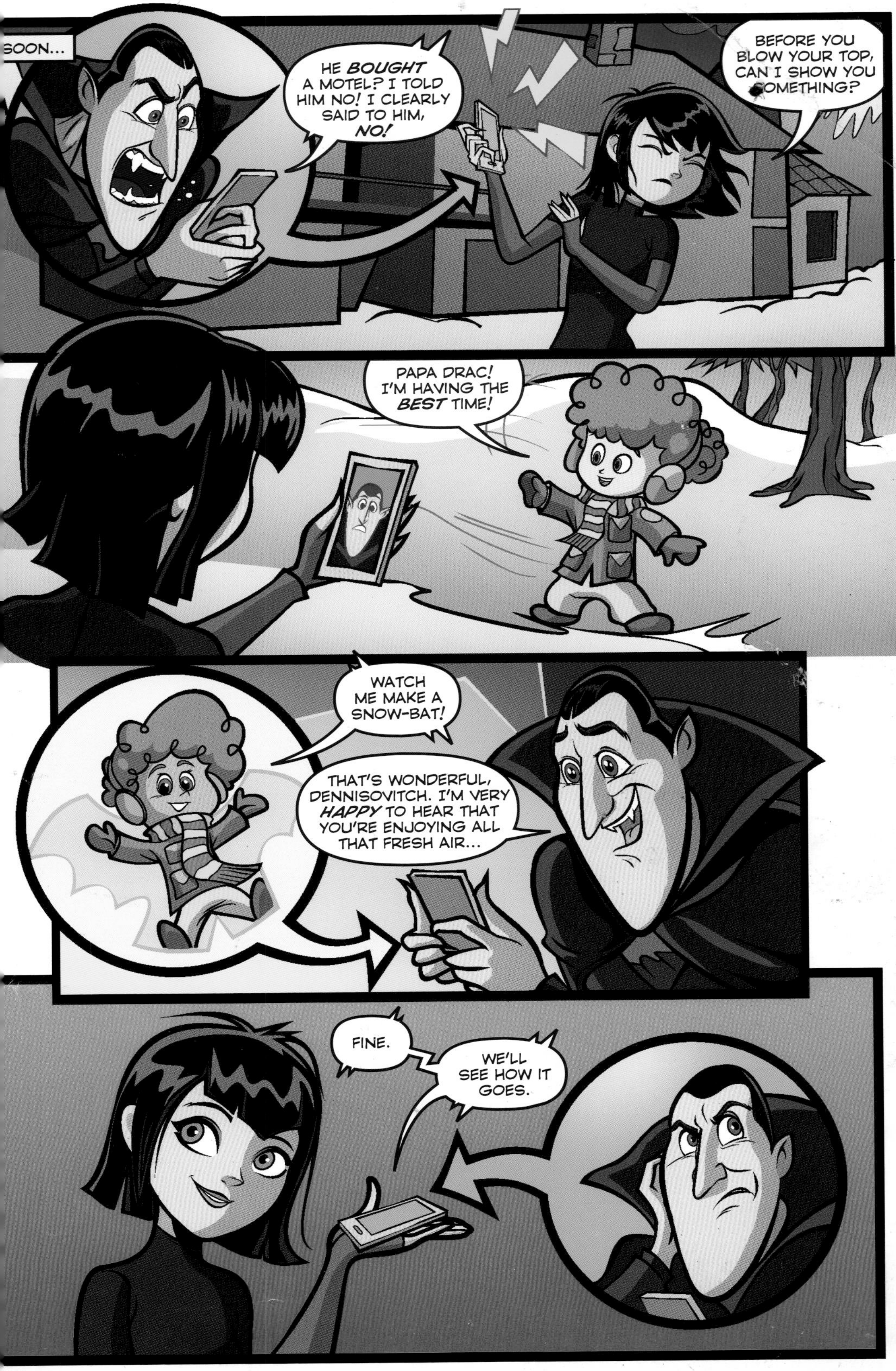
SOON...
HE BOUGHT A MOTEL? I TOLD HIM NO! I CLEARLY SAID TO HIM, NO!
BEFORE YOU BLOW YOUR TOP, CAN I SHOW YOU SOMETHING?
PAPA DRAC! I'M HAVING THE BEST TIME!
WATCH ME MAKE A SNOW-BAT!
THAT'S WONDERFUL, DENNISOVITCH. I'M VERY HAPPY TO HEAR THAT YOU'RE ENJOYING ALL THAT FRESH AIR...
FINE.
WE'LL SEE HOW IT GOES.

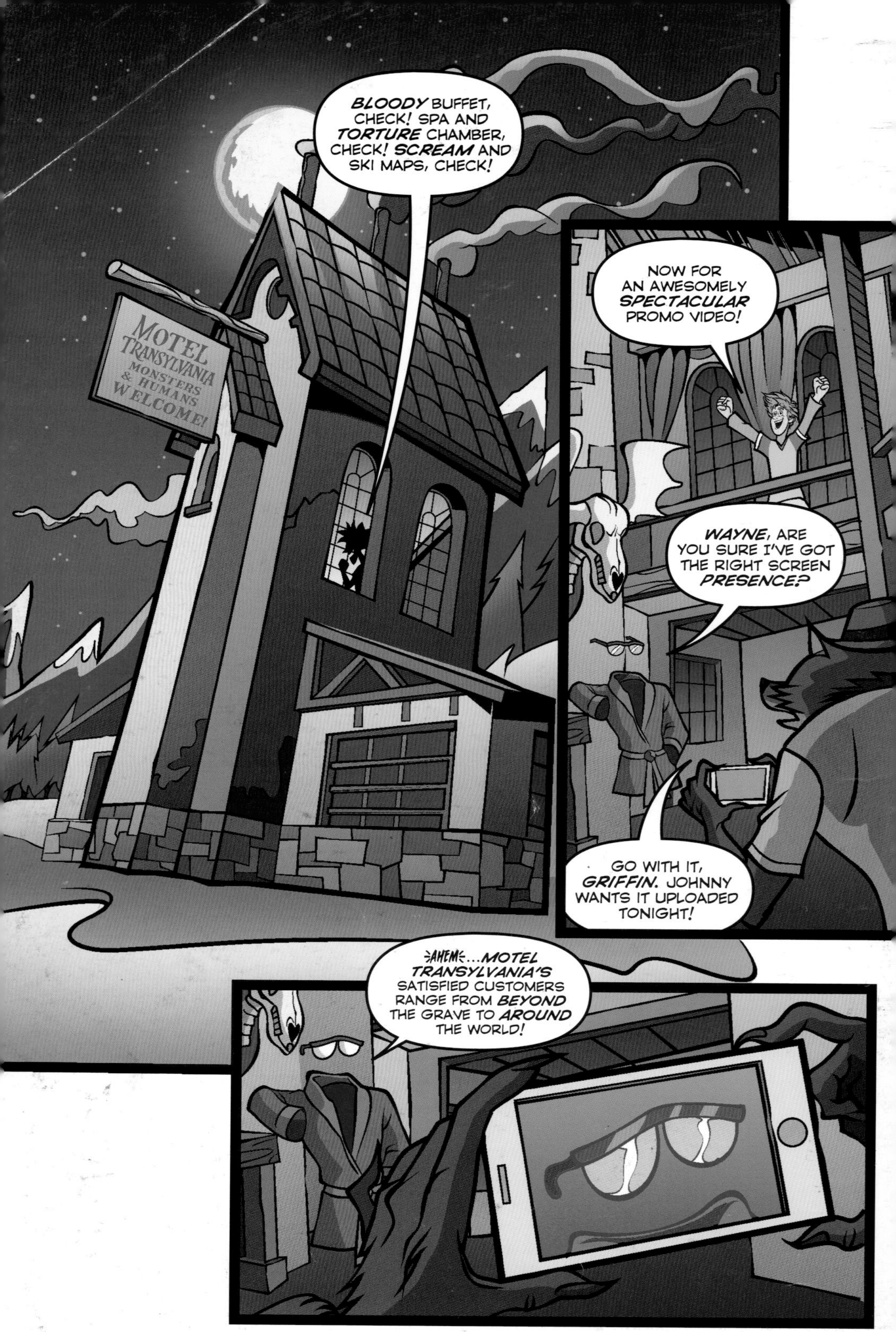
BLOODY BUFFET, CHECK! SPA AND TORTURE CHAMBER, CHECK! SCREAM AND SKI MAPS, CHECK!
MOTEL TRANSYLVANIA MONSTERS & HUMANS WELCOME!
NOW FOR AN AWESOMELY SPECTACULAR PROMO VIDEO!
WAYNE, ARE YOU SURE I'VE GOT THE RIGHT SCREEN PRESENCE?
GO WITH IT, GRIFFIN. JOHNNY WANTS IT UPLOADED TONIGHT!
AHEM...MOTEL TRANSYLVANIA'S SATISFIED CUSTOMERS RANGE FROM BEYOND THE GRAVE TO AROUND THE WORLD!

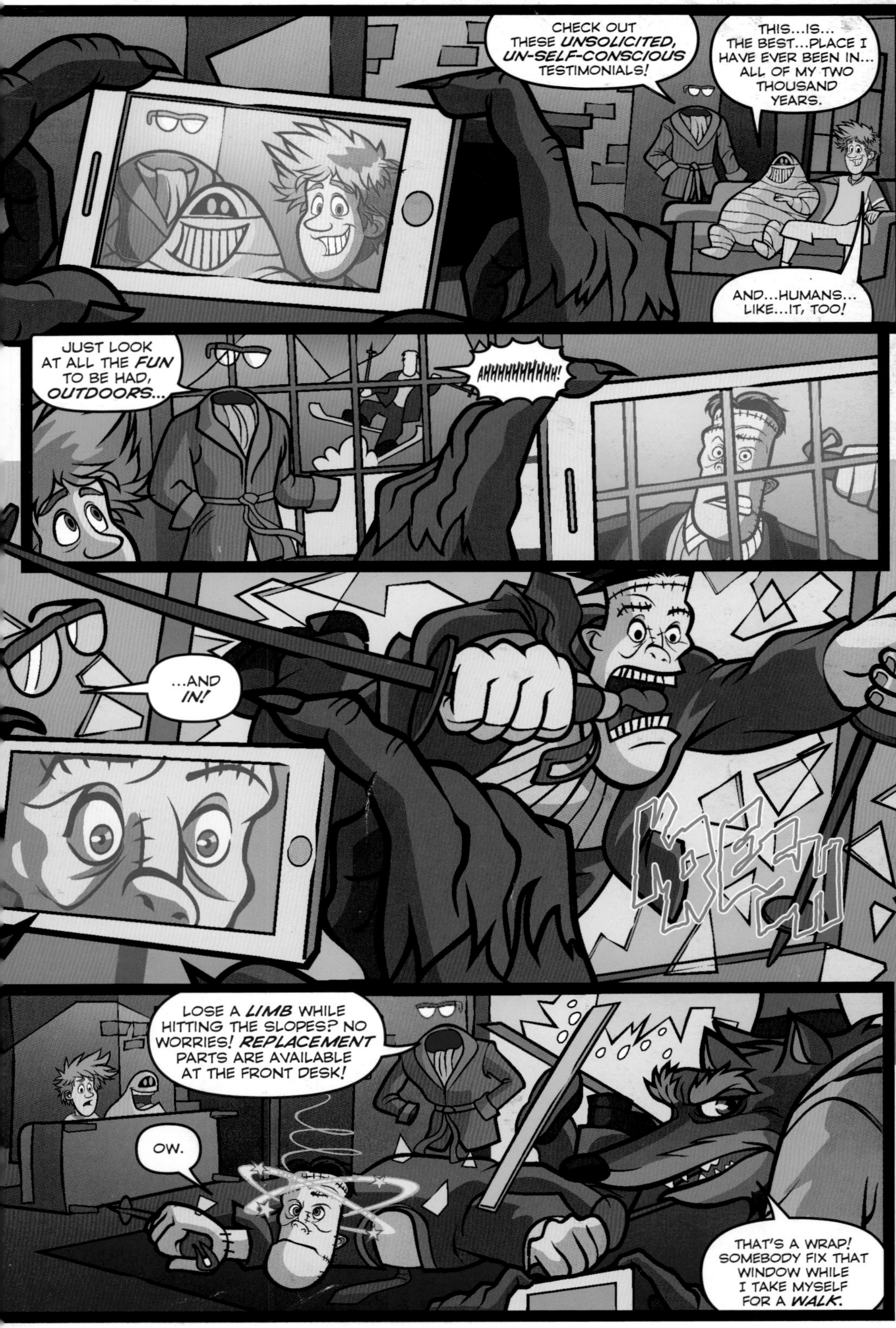
CHECK OUT THESE UNSOLICITED, UN-SELF-CONSCIOUS TESTIMONIALS!
THIS...IS... THE BEST...PLACE I HAVE EVER BEEN IN... ALL OF MY TWO THOUSAND YEARS.
AND...HUMANS... LIKE...IT, TOO!
JUST LOOK AT ALL THE FUN TO BE HAD, OUTDOORS...
AHHHHHHHHHH!
...AND IN!
LOSE A LIMB WHILE HITTING THE SLOPES? NO WORRIES! REPLACEMENT PARTS ARE AVAILABLE AT THE FRONT DESK!
OW.
THAT'S A WRAP! SOMEBODY FIX THAT WINDOW WHILE I TAKE MYSELF FOR A WALK.

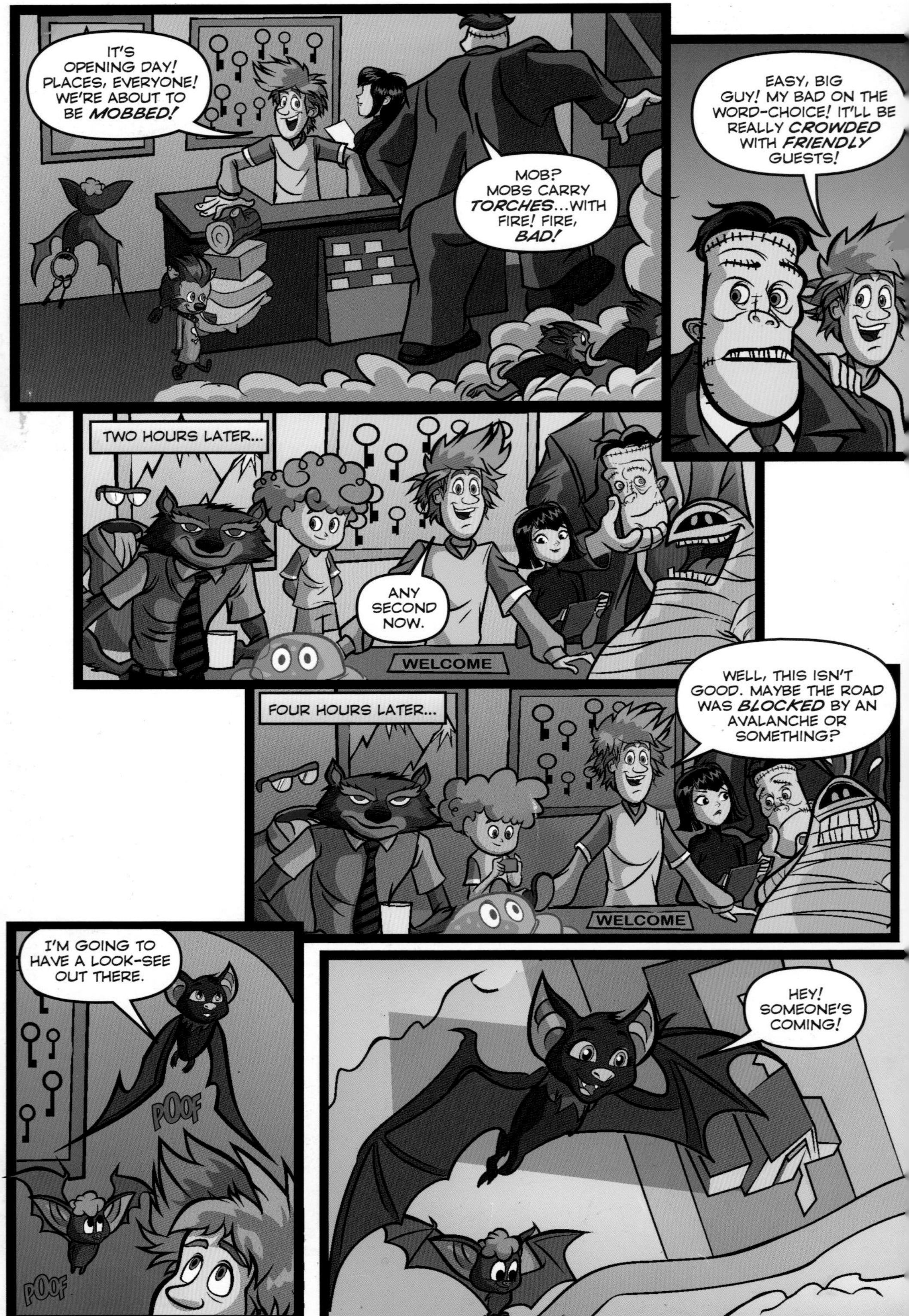
IT'S OPENING DAY! PLACES, EVERYONE! WE'RE ABOUT TO BE *MOBBED!*
MOB? MOBS CARRY *TORCHES*...WITH FIRE! FIRE, *BAD!*
EASY, BIG GUY! MY BAD ON THE WORD-CHOICE! IT'LL BE REALLY *CROWDED* WITH *FRIENDLY* GUESTS!
TWO HOURS LATER...
ANY SECOND NOW.
WELCOME
FOUR HOURS LATER...
WELL, THIS ISN'T GOOD. MAYBE THE ROAD WAS *BLOCKED* BY AN AVALANCHE OR SOMETHING?
WELCOME
I'M GOING TO HAVE A LOOK-SEE OUT THERE.
POOF
POOF
HEY! SOMEONE'S COMING!

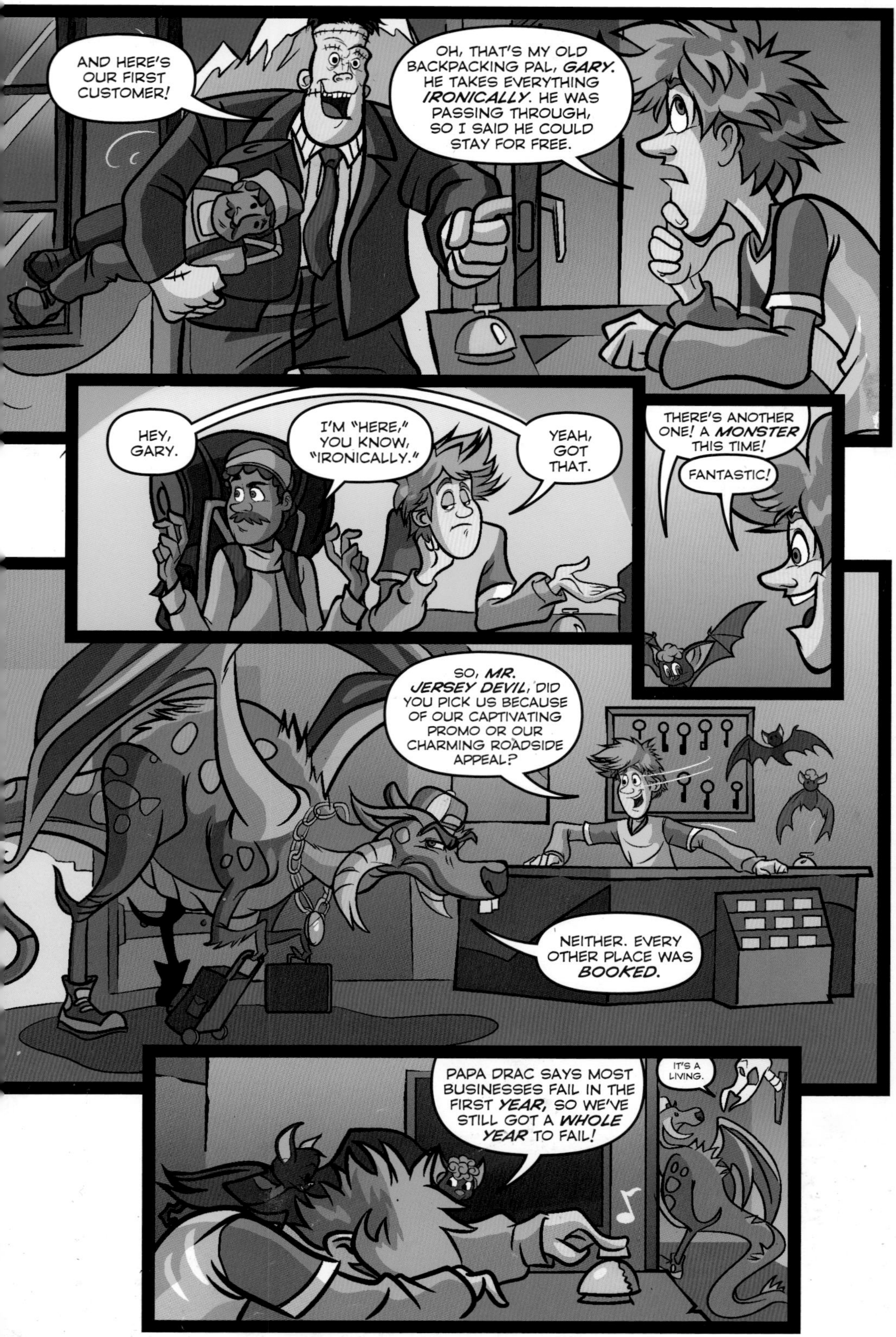
AND HERE'S OUR FIRST CUSTOMER!
OH, THAT'S MY OLD BACKPACKING PAL, GARY. HE TAKES EVERYTHING IRONICALLY. HE WAS PASSING THROUGH, SO I SAID HE COULD STAY FOR FREE.
HEY, GARY.
I'M "HERE," YOU KNOW, "IRONICALLY."
YEAH, GOT THAT.
THERE'S ANOTHER ONE! A MONSTER THIS TIME!
FANTASTIC!
SO, MR. JERSEY DEVIL, DID YOU PICK US BECAUSE OF OUR CAPTIVATING PROMO OR OUR CHARMING ROADSIDE APPEAL?
NEITHER. EVERY OTHER PLACE WAS BOOKED.
PAPA DRAC SAYS MOST BUSINESSES FAIL IN THE FIRST YEAR, SO WE'VE STILL GOT A WHOLE YEAR TO FAIL!
IT'S A LIVING.

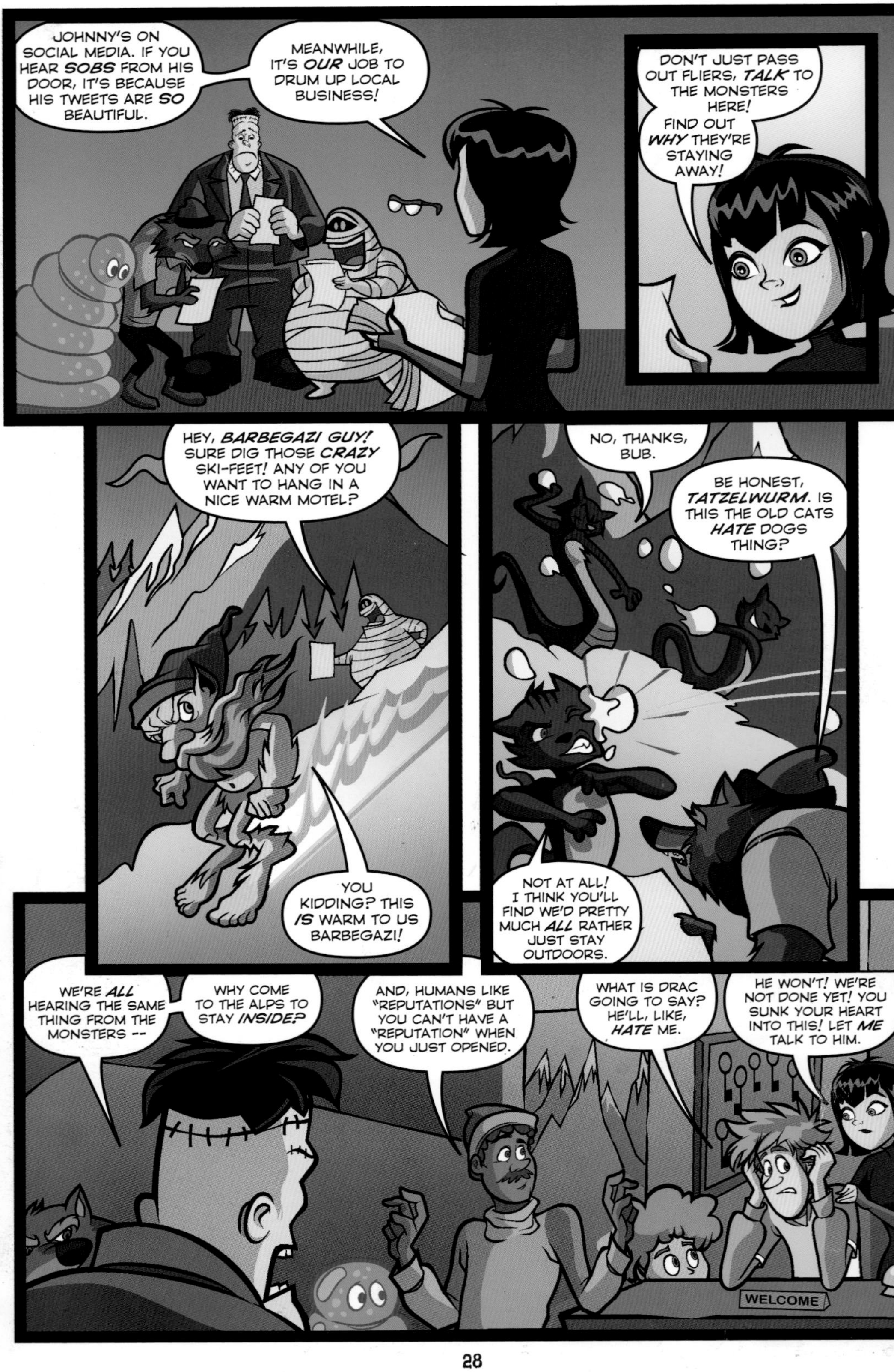
JOHNNY'S ON SOCIAL MEDIA. IF YOU HEAR SOBS FROM HIS DOOR, IT'S BECAUSE HIS TWEETS ARE SO BEAUTIFUL.
MEANWHILE, IT'S OUR JOB TO DRUM UP LOCAL BUSINESS!
DON'T JUST PASS OUT FLIERS, TALK TO THE MONSTERS HERE!
FIND OUT WHY THEY'RE STAYING AWAY!
HEY, BARBEGAZI GUY! SURE DIG THOSE CRAZY SKI-FEET! ANY OF YOU WANT TO HANG IN A NICE WARM MOTEL?
YOU KIDDING? THIS IS WARM TO US BARBEGAZI!
NO, THANKS, BUB.
BE HONEST, TATZELWURM. IS THIS THE OLD CATS HATE DOGS THING?
NOT AT ALL! I THINK YOU'LL FIND WE'D PRETTY MUCH ALL RATHER JUST STAY OUTDOORS.
WE'RE ALL HEARING THE SAME THING FROM THE MONSTERS --
WHY COME TO THE ALPS TO STAY INSIDE?
AND, HUMANS LIKE "REPUTATIONS" BUT YOU CAN'T HAVE A "REPUTATION" WHEN YOU JUST OPENED.
WHAT IS DRAC GOING TO SAY? HE'LL, LIKE, HATE ME.
HE WON'T! WE'RE NOT DONE YET! YOU SUNK YOUR HEART INTO THIS! LET ME TALK TO HIM.
WELCOME

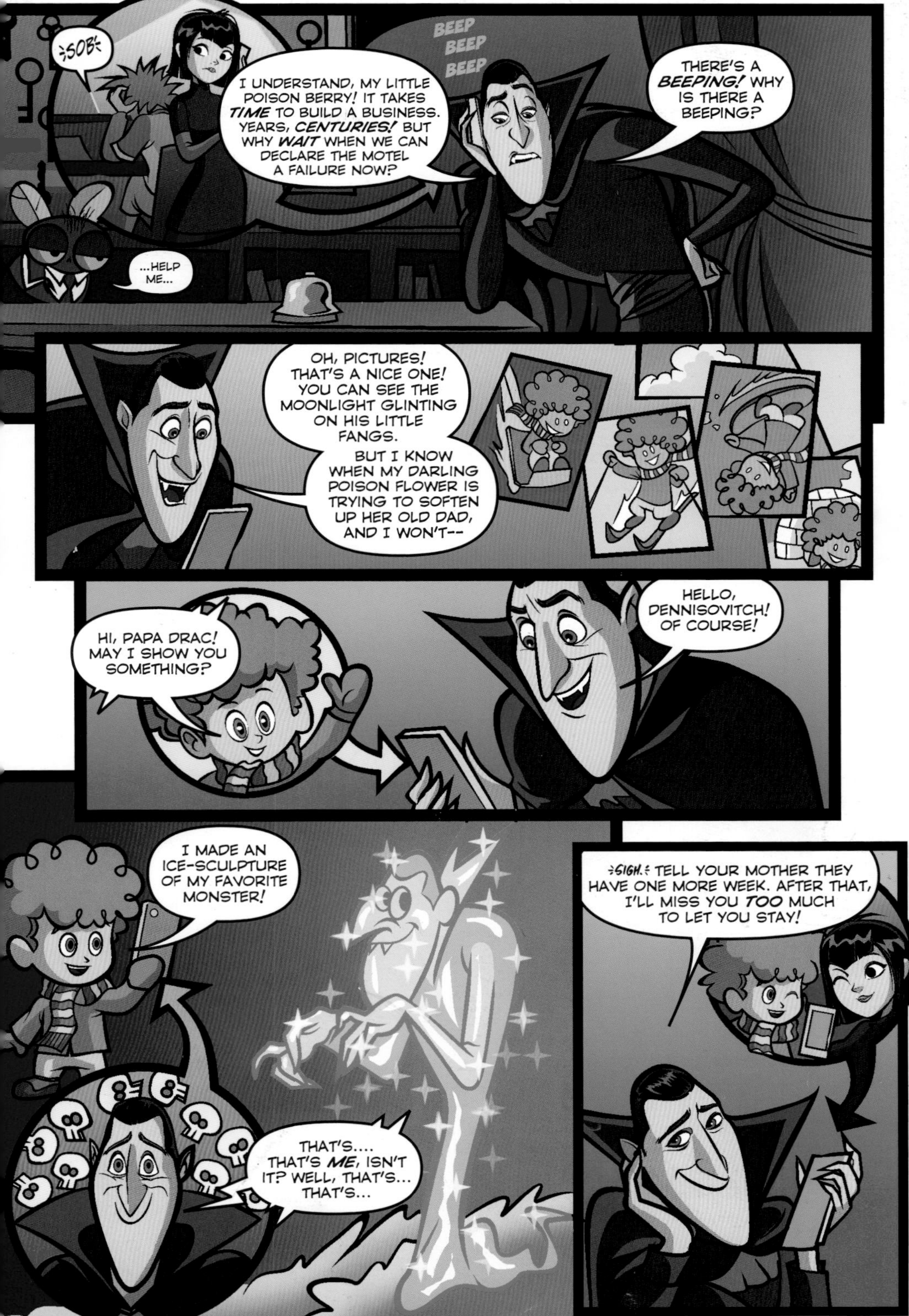

SOB
I UNDERSTAND, MY LITTLE POISON BERRY! IT TAKES *TIME* TO BUILD A BUSINESS. YEARS, *CENTURIES!* BUT WHY *WAIT* WHEN WE CAN DECLARE THE MOTEL A FAILURE NOW?
BEEP BEEP BEEP
THERE'S A *BEEPING!* WHY IS THERE A BEEPING?
...HELP ME...
OH, PICTURES! THAT'S A NICE ONE! YOU CAN SEE THE MOONLIGHT GLINTING ON HIS LITTLE FANGS.
BUT I KNOW WHEN MY DARLING POISON FLOWER IS TRYING TO SOFTEN UP HER OLD DAD, AND I WON'T--
HI, PAPA DRAC! MAY I SHOW YOU SOMETHING?
HELLO, DENNISOVITCH! OF COURSE!
I MADE AN ICE-SCULPTURE OF MY FAVORITE MONSTER!
THAT'S.... THAT'S *ME*, ISN'T IT? WELL, THAT'S... THAT'S...
SIGH. TELL YOUR MOTHER THEY HAVE ONE MORE WEEK. AFTER THAT, I'LL MISS YOU *TOO* MUCH TO LET YOU STAY!

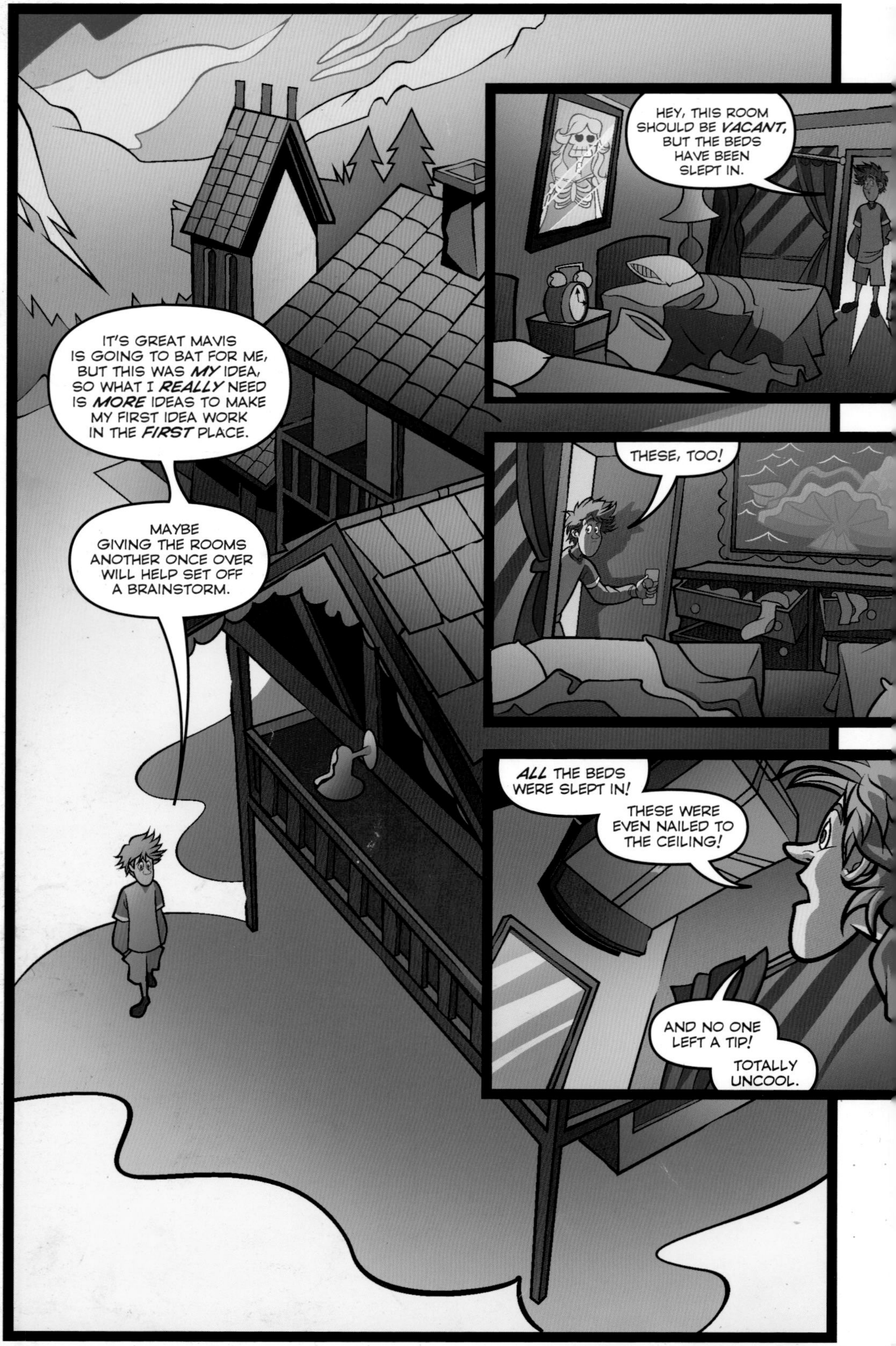
IT'S GREAT MAVIS IS GOING TO BAT FOR ME, BUT THIS WAS *MY* IDEA, SO WHAT I *REALLY* NEED IS *MORE* IDEAS TO MAKE MY FIRST IDEA WORK IN THE *FIRST* PLACE.
MAYBE GIVING THE ROOMS ANOTHER ONCE OVER WILL HELP SET OFF A BRAINSTORM.
HEY, THIS ROOM SHOULD BE *VACANT,* BUT THE BEDS HAVE BEEN SLEPT IN.
THESE, TOO!
ALL THE BEDS WERE SLEPT IN!
THESE WERE EVEN NAILED TO THE CEILING!
AND NO ONE LEFT A TIP!
TOTALLY UNCOOL.

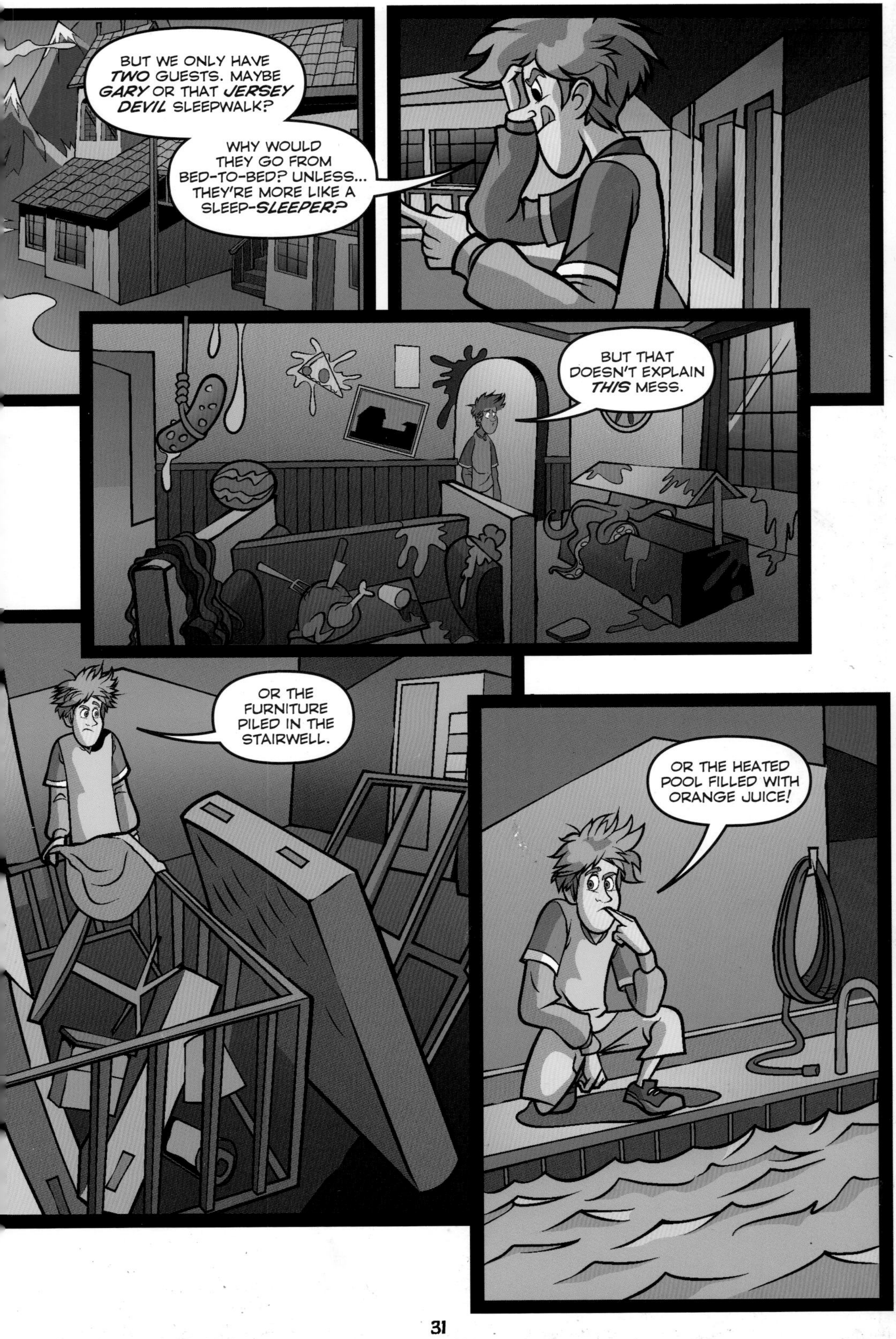
BUT WE ONLY HAVE TWO GUESTS. MAYBE GARY OR THAT JERSEY DEVIL SLEEPWALK?
WHY WOULD THEY GO FROM BED-TO-BED? UNLESS... THEY'RE MORE LIKE A SLEEP-SLEEPER?
BUT THAT DOESN'T EXPLAIN THIS MESS.
OR THE FURNITURE PILED IN THE STAIRWELL.
OR THE HEATED POOL FILLED WITH ORANGE JUICE!

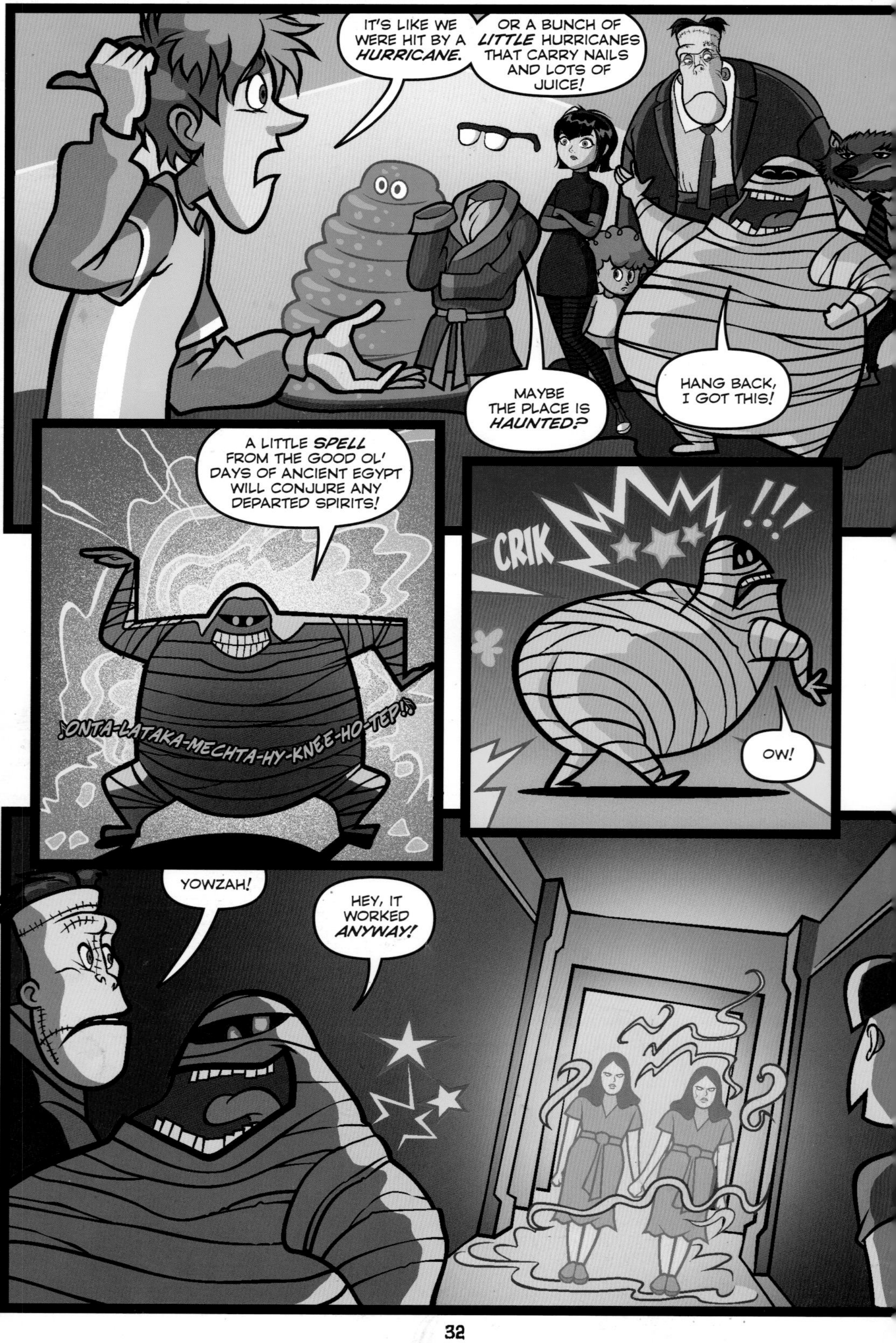
IT'S LIKE WE WERE HIT BY A HURRICANE.
OR A BUNCH OF LITTLE HURRICANES THAT CARRY NAILS AND LOTS OF JUICE!
MAYBE THE PLACE IS HAUNTED?
HANG BACK, I GOT THIS!
A LITTLE SPELL FROM THE GOOD OL' DAYS OF ANCIENT EGYPT WILL CONJURE ANY DEPARTED SPIRITS!
¡ONTA-LATAKA-MECHTA-HY-KNEE-HO-TEP!¡
CRIK
!!!
OW!
YOWZAH!
HEY, IT WORKED ANYWAY!

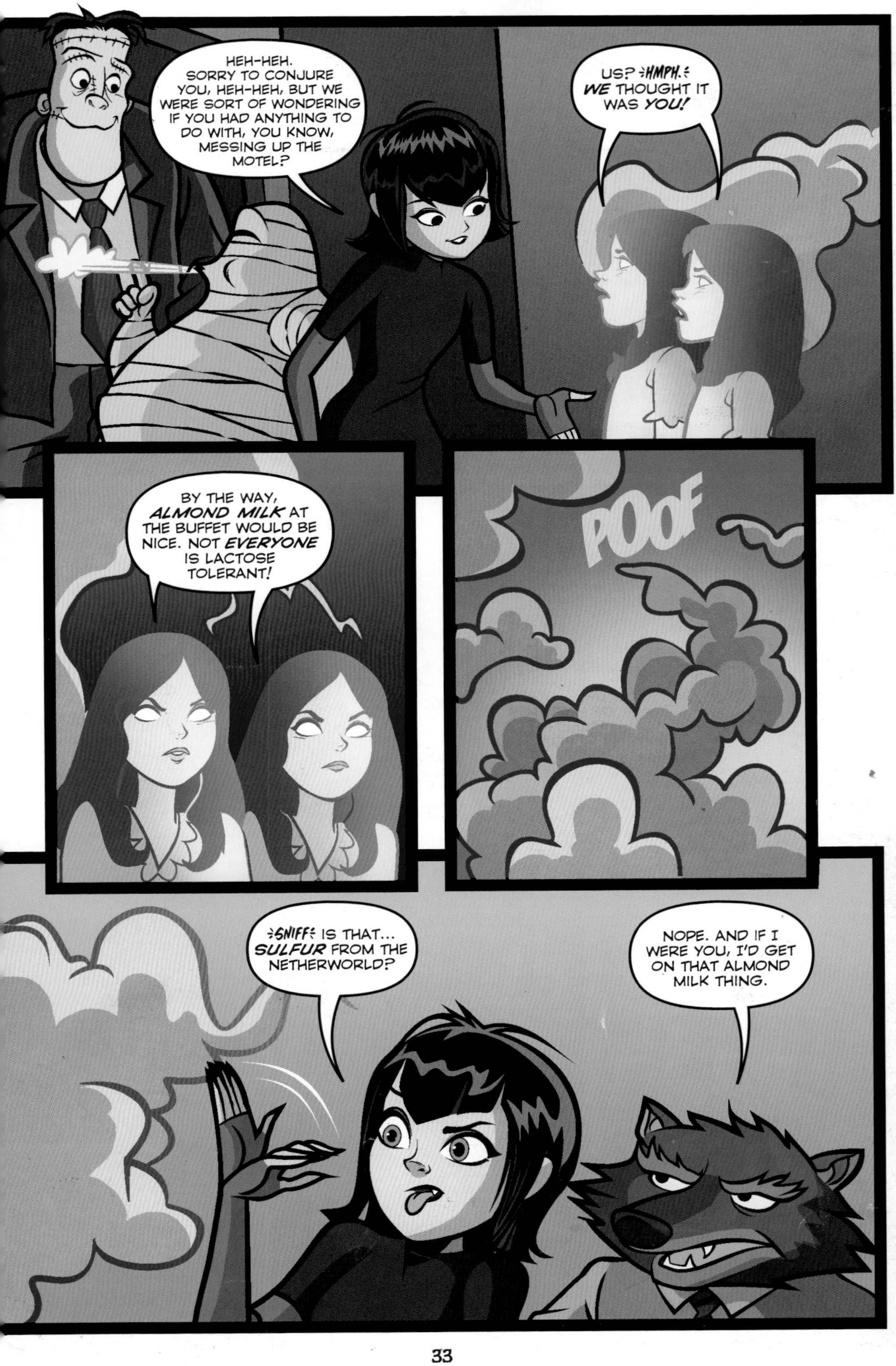
HEH-HEH. SORRY TO CONJURE YOU, HEH-HEH, BUT WE WERE SORT OF WONDERING IF YOU HAD ANYTHING TO DO WITH, YOU KNOW, MESSING UP THE MOTEL?
US? HMPH. WE THOUGHT IT WAS YOU!
BY THE WAY, ALMOND MILK AT THE BUFFET WOULD BE NICE. NOT EVERYONE IS LACTOSE TOLERANT!
POOF
SNIFF IS THAT... SULFUR FROM THE NETHERWORLD?
NOPE. AND IF I WERE YOU, I'D GET ON THAT ALMOND MILK THING.

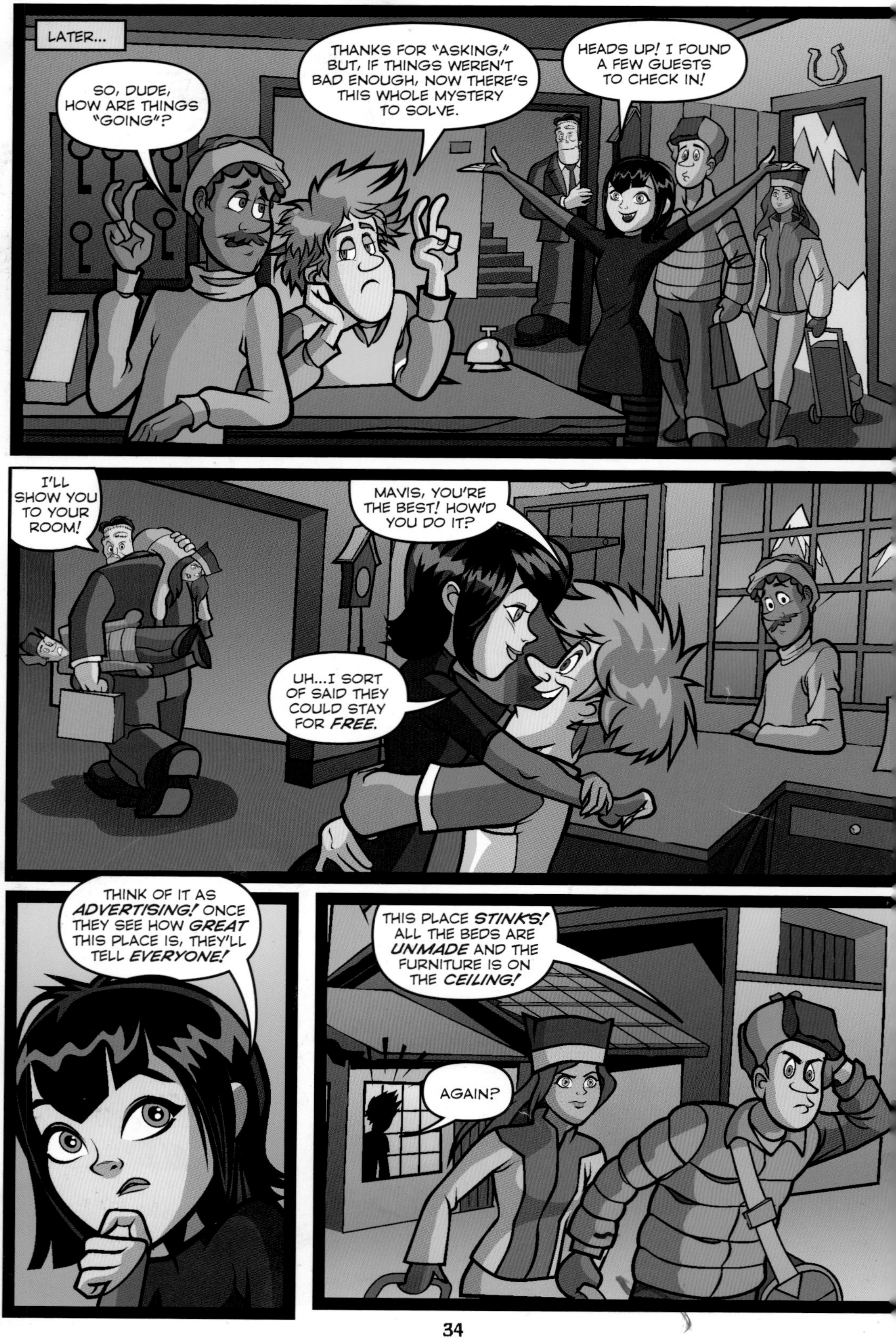
LATER...
SO, DUDE, HOW ARE THINGS "GOING"?
THANKS FOR "ASKING," BUT, IF THINGS WEREN'T BAD ENOUGH, NOW THERE'S THIS WHOLE MYSTERY TO SOLVE.
HEADS UP! I FOUND A FEW GUESTS TO CHECK IN!
I'LL SHOW YOU TO YOUR ROOM!
MAVIS, YOU'RE THE BEST! HOW'D YOU DO IT?
UH...I SORT OF SAID THEY COULD STAY FOR FREE.
THINK OF IT AS ADVERTISING! ONCE THEY SEE HOW GREAT THIS PLACE IS, THEY'LL TELL EVERYONE!
THIS PLACE STINKS! ALL THE BEDS ARE UNMADE AND THE FURNITURE IS ON THE CEILING!
AGAIN?

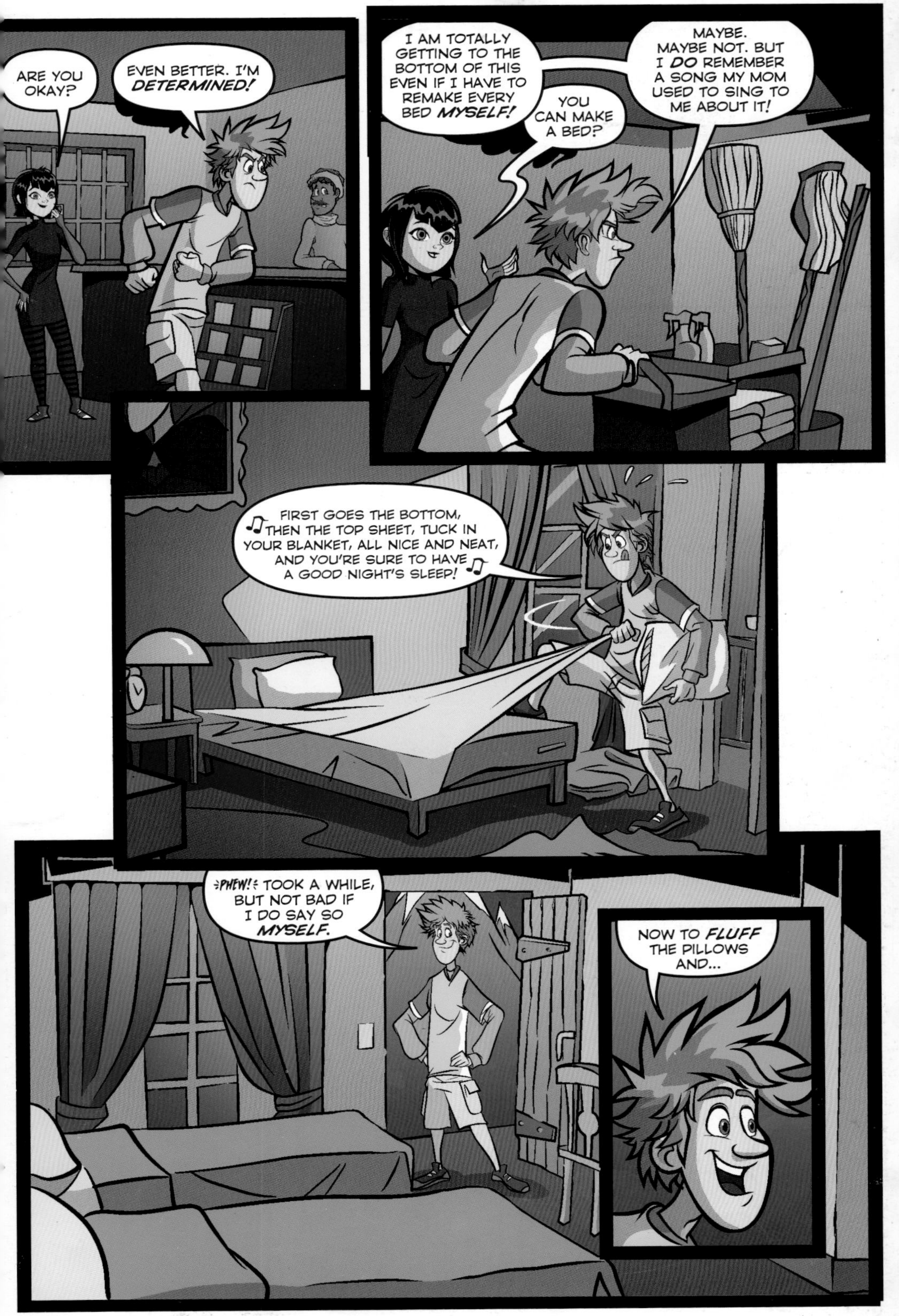
ARE YOU OKAY?
EVEN BETTER. I'M DETERMINED!
I AM TOTALLY GETTING TO THE BOTTOM OF THIS EVEN IF I HAVE TO REMAKE EVERY BED MYSELF!
YOU CAN MAKE A BED?
MAYBE. MAYBE NOT. BUT I DO REMEMBER A SONG MY MOM USED TO SING TO ME ABOUT IT!
♫ FIRST GOES THE BOTTOM, THEN THE TOP SHEET, TUCK IN YOUR BLANKET, ALL NICE AND NEAT, AND YOU'RE SURE TO HAVE A GOOD NIGHT'S SLEEP! ♫
PHEW! TOOK A WHILE, BUT NOT BAD IF I DO SAY SO MYSELF.
NOW TO FLUFF THE PILLOWS AND...

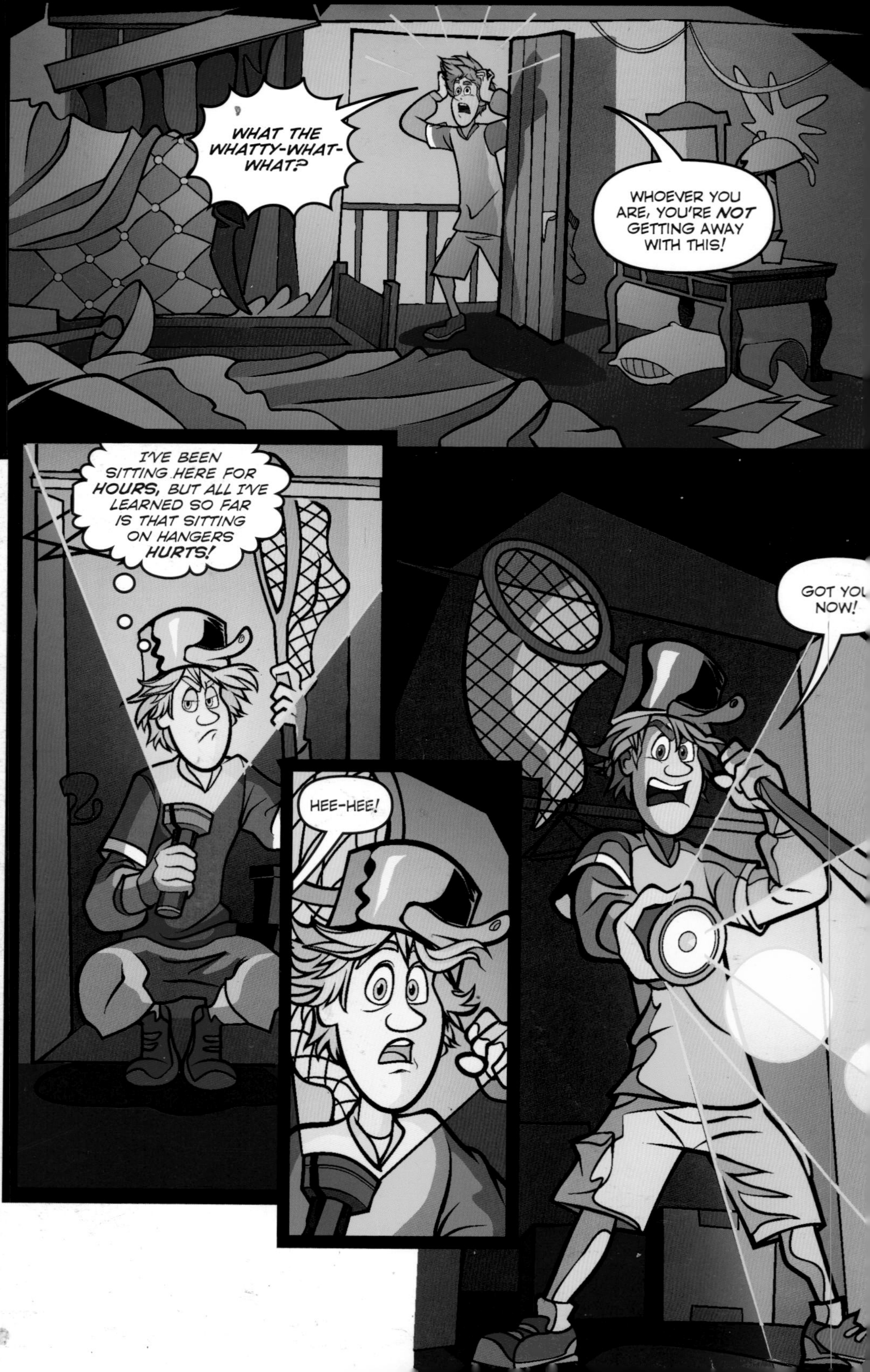

WHAT THE WHATTY-WHAT-WHAT?
WHOEVER YOU ARE, YOU'RE NOT GETTING AWAY WITH THIS!
I'VE BEEN SITTING HERE FOR HOURS, BUT ALL I'VE LEARNED SO FAR IS THAT SITTING ON HANGERS HURTS!
HEE-HEE!
GOT YOU NOW!

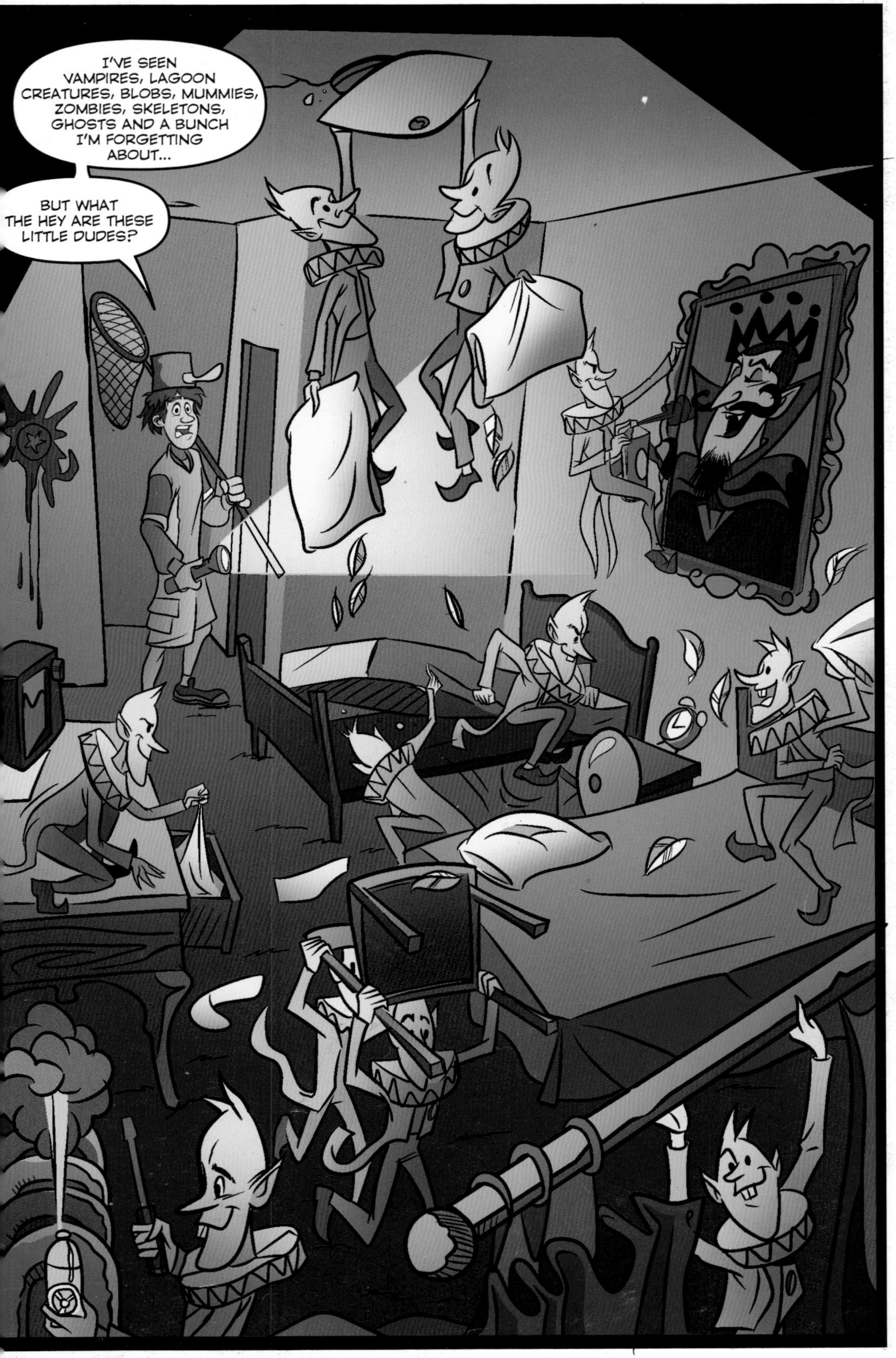
I'VE SEEN VAMPIRES, LAGOON CREATURES, BLOBS, MUMMIES, ZOMBIES, SKELETONS, GHOSTS AND A BUNCH I'M FORGETTING ABOUT...
BUT WHAT THE HEY ARE THESE LITTLE DUDES?

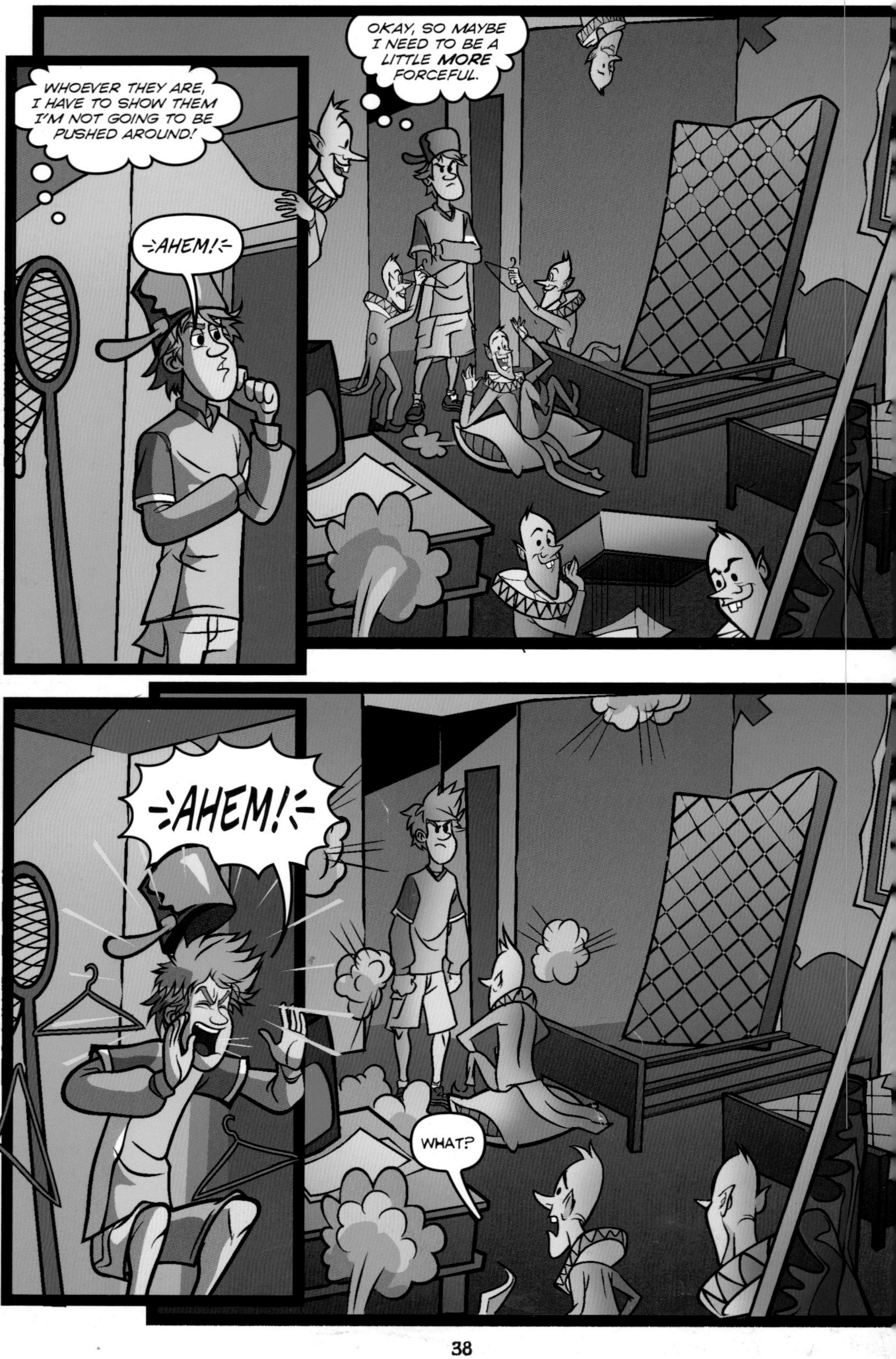
WHOEVER THEY ARE, I HAVE TO SHOW THEM I'M NOT GOING TO BE PUSHED AROUND!
-AHEM!-
OKAY, SO MAYBE I NEED TO BE A LITTLE MORE FORCEFUL.
-AHEM!-
WHAT?

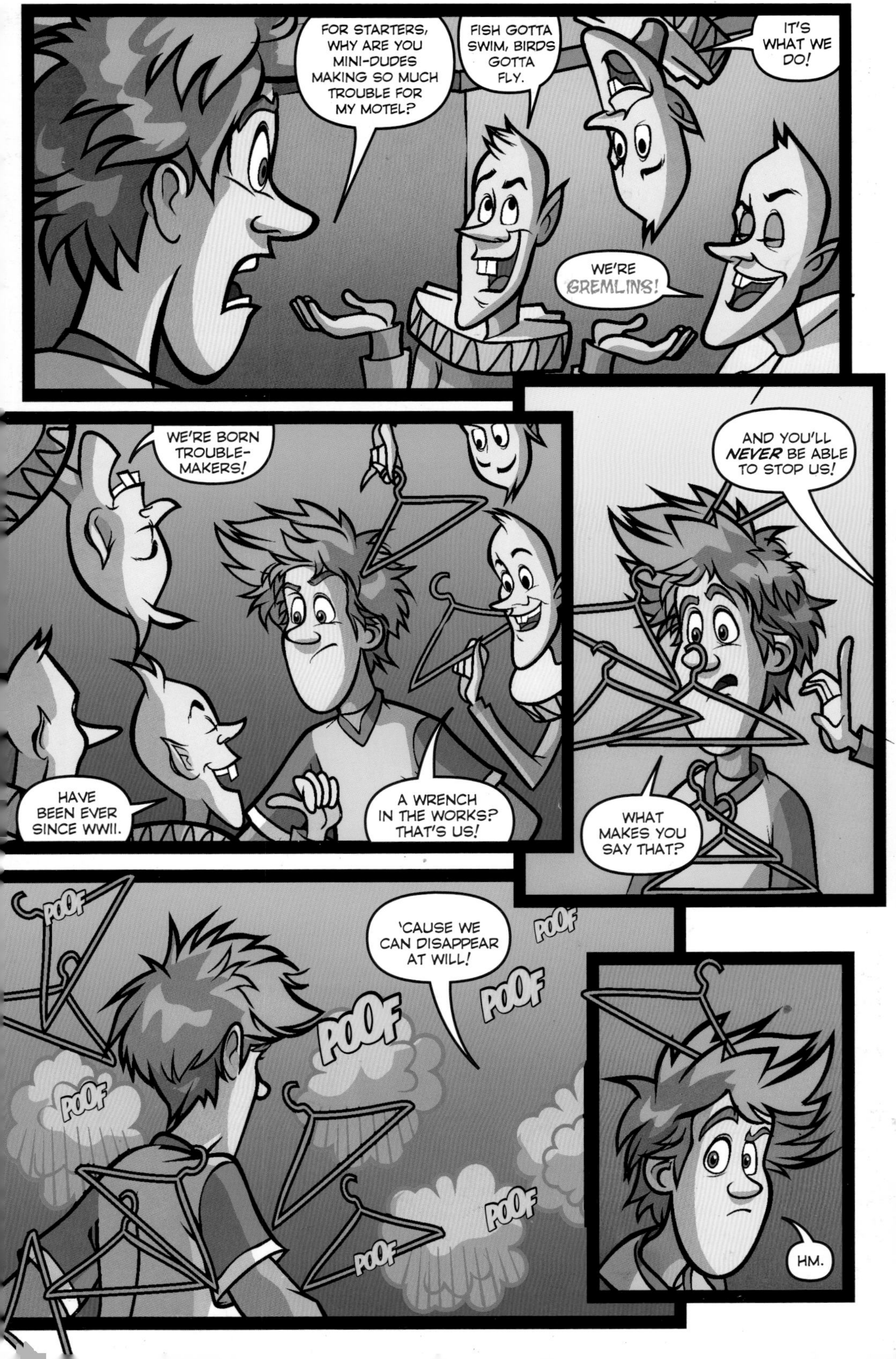
FOR STARTERS, WHY ARE YOU MINI-DUDES MAKING SO MUCH TROUBLE FOR MY MOTEL?
FISH GOTTA SWIM, BIRDS GOTTA FLY.
IT'S WHAT WE DO!
WE'RE GREMLINS!
WE'RE BORN TROUBLE-MAKERS!
HAVE BEEN EVER SINCE WWII.
A WRENCH IN THE WORKS? THAT'S US!
AND YOU'LL NEVER BE ABLE TO STOP US!
WHAT MAKES YOU SAY THAT?
'CAUSE WE CAN DISAPPEAR AT WILL!
POOF
POOF
POOF
POOF
POOF
POOF
POOF
HM.

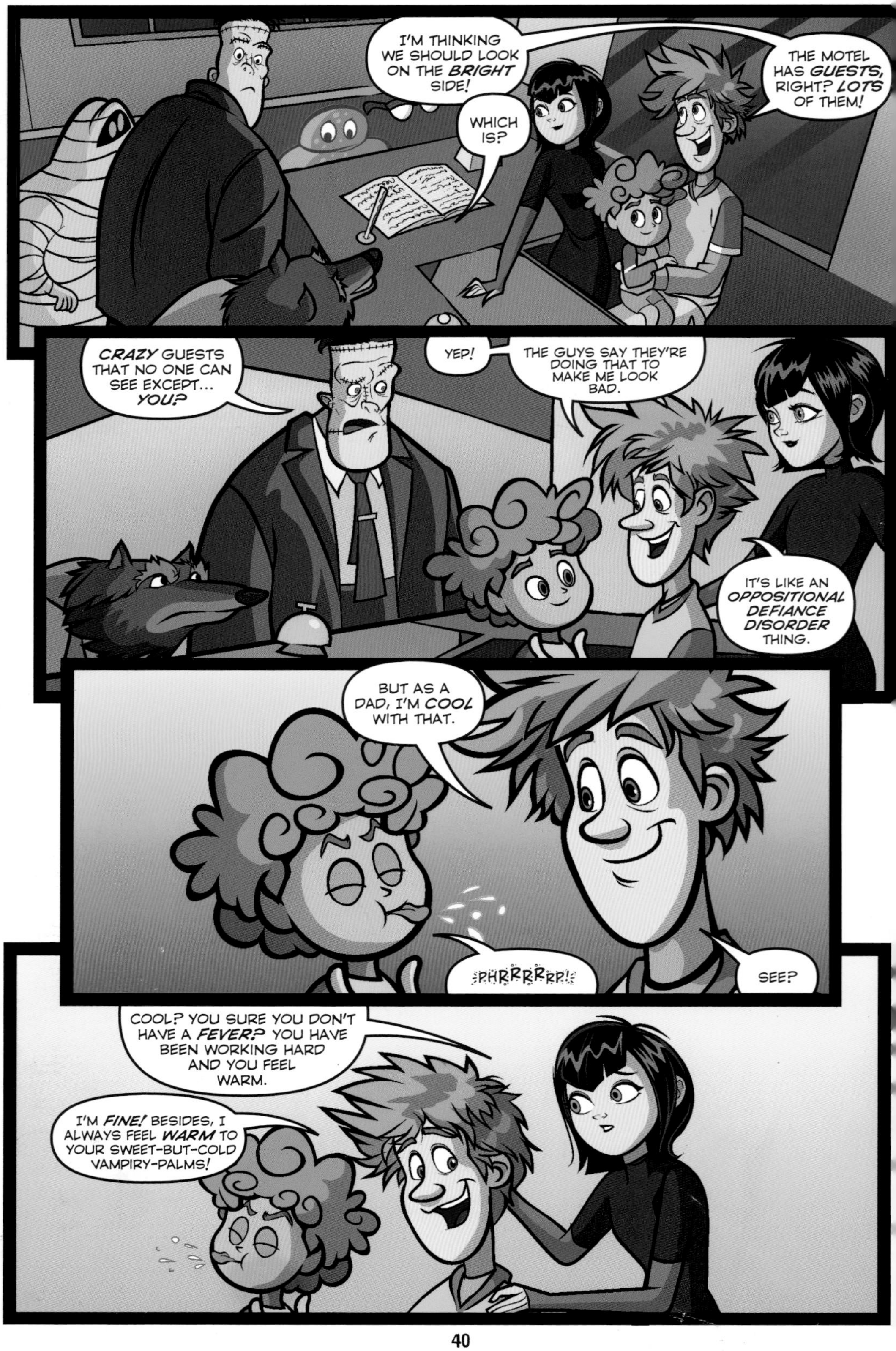
I'M THINKING WE SHOULD LOOK ON THE *BRIGHT* SIDE!
WHICH IS?
THE MOTEL HAS *GUESTS,* RIGHT? *LOTS* OF THEM!
CRAZY GUESTS THAT NO ONE CAN SEE EXCEPT... *YOU?*
YEP!
THE GUYS SAY THEY'RE DOING THAT TO MAKE ME LOOK BAD.
IT'S LIKE AN *OPPOSITIONAL DEFIANCE DISORDER* THING.
BUT AS A DAD, I'M *COOL* WITH THAT.
PHRRRRRP!
SEE?
COOL? YOU SURE YOU DON'T HAVE A *FEVER?* YOU HAVE BEEN WORKING HARD AND YOU FEEL WARM.
I'M *FINE!* BESIDES, I ALWAYS FEEL *WARM* TO YOUR SWEET-BUT-COLD VAMPIRY-PALMS!

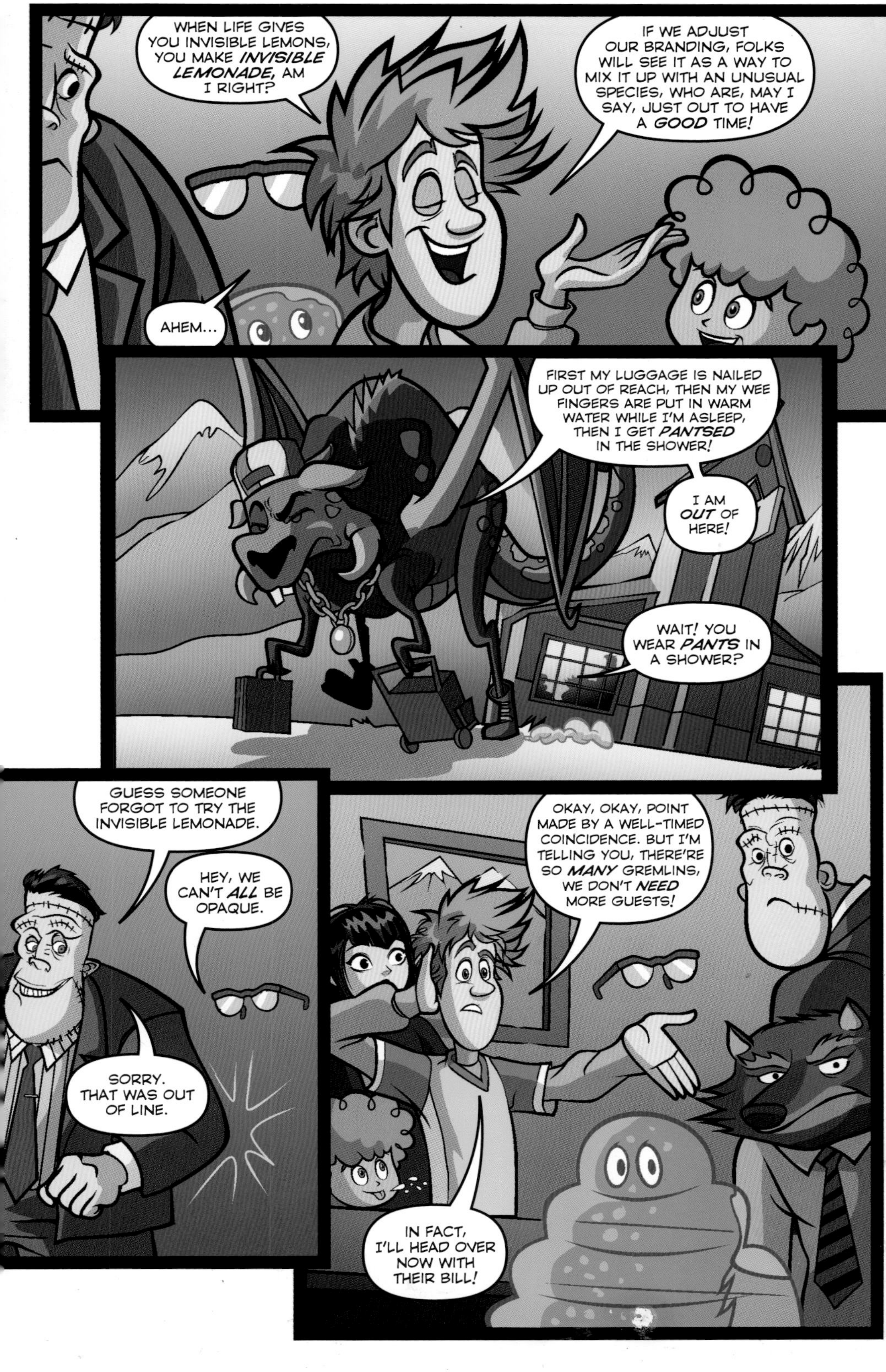
WHEN LIFE GIVES YOU INVISIBLE LEMONS, YOU MAKE INVISIBLE LEMONADE, AM I RIGHT?
IF WE ADJUST OUR BRANDING, FOLKS WILL SEE IT AS A WAY TO MIX IT UP WITH AN UNUSUAL SPECIES, WHO ARE, MAY I SAY, JUST OUT TO HAVE A GOOD TIME!
AHEM...
FIRST MY LUGGAGE IS NAILED UP OUT OF REACH, THEN MY WEE FINGERS ARE PUT IN WARM WATER WHILE I'M ASLEEP, THEN I GET PANTSED IN THE SHOWER!
I AM OUT OF HERE!
WAIT! YOU WEAR PANTS IN A SHOWER?
GUESS SOMEONE FORGOT TO TRY THE INVISIBLE LEMONADE.
HEY, WE CAN'T ALL BE OPAQUE.
SORRY. THAT WAS OUT OF LINE.
OKAY, OKAY, POINT MADE BY A WELL-TIMED COINCIDENCE. BUT I'M TELLING YOU, THERE'RE SO MANY GREMLINS, WE DON'T NEED MORE GUESTS!
IN FACT, I'LL HEAD OVER NOW WITH THEIR BILL!

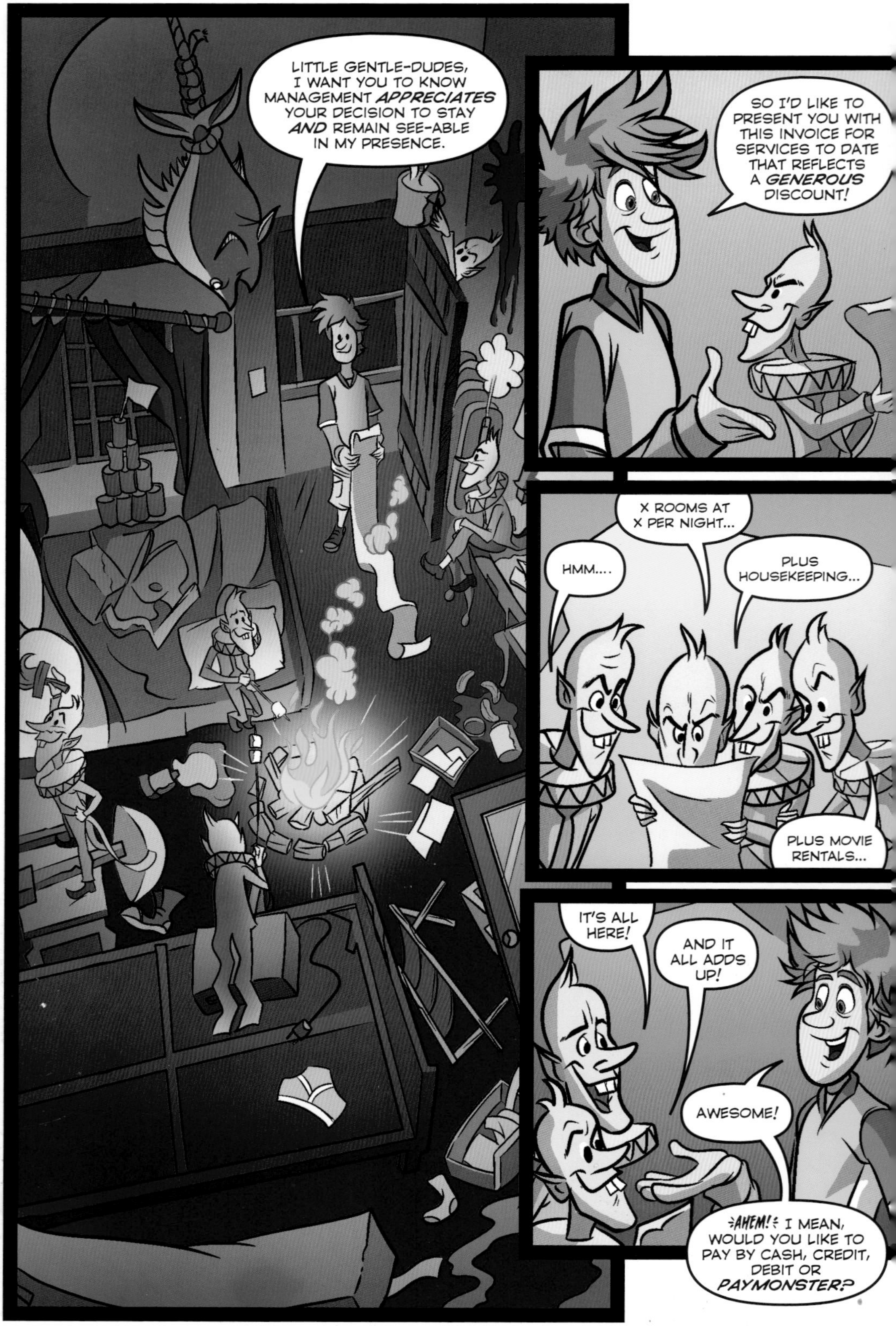

LITTLE GENTLE-DUDES, I WANT YOU TO KNOW MANAGEMENT APPRECIATES YOUR DECISION TO STAY AND REMAIN SEE-ABLE IN MY PRESENCE.
SO I'D LIKE TO PRESENT YOU WITH THIS INVOICE FOR SERVICES TO DATE THAT REFLECTS A GENEROUS DISCOUNT!
X ROOMS AT X PER NIGHT...
HMM....
PLUS HOUSEKEEPING...
PLUS MOVIE RENTALS...
IT'S ALL HERE!
AND IT ALL ADDS UP!
AWESOME!
AHEM! I MEAN, WOULD YOU LIKE TO PAY BY CASH, CREDIT, DEBIT OR PAYMONSTER?

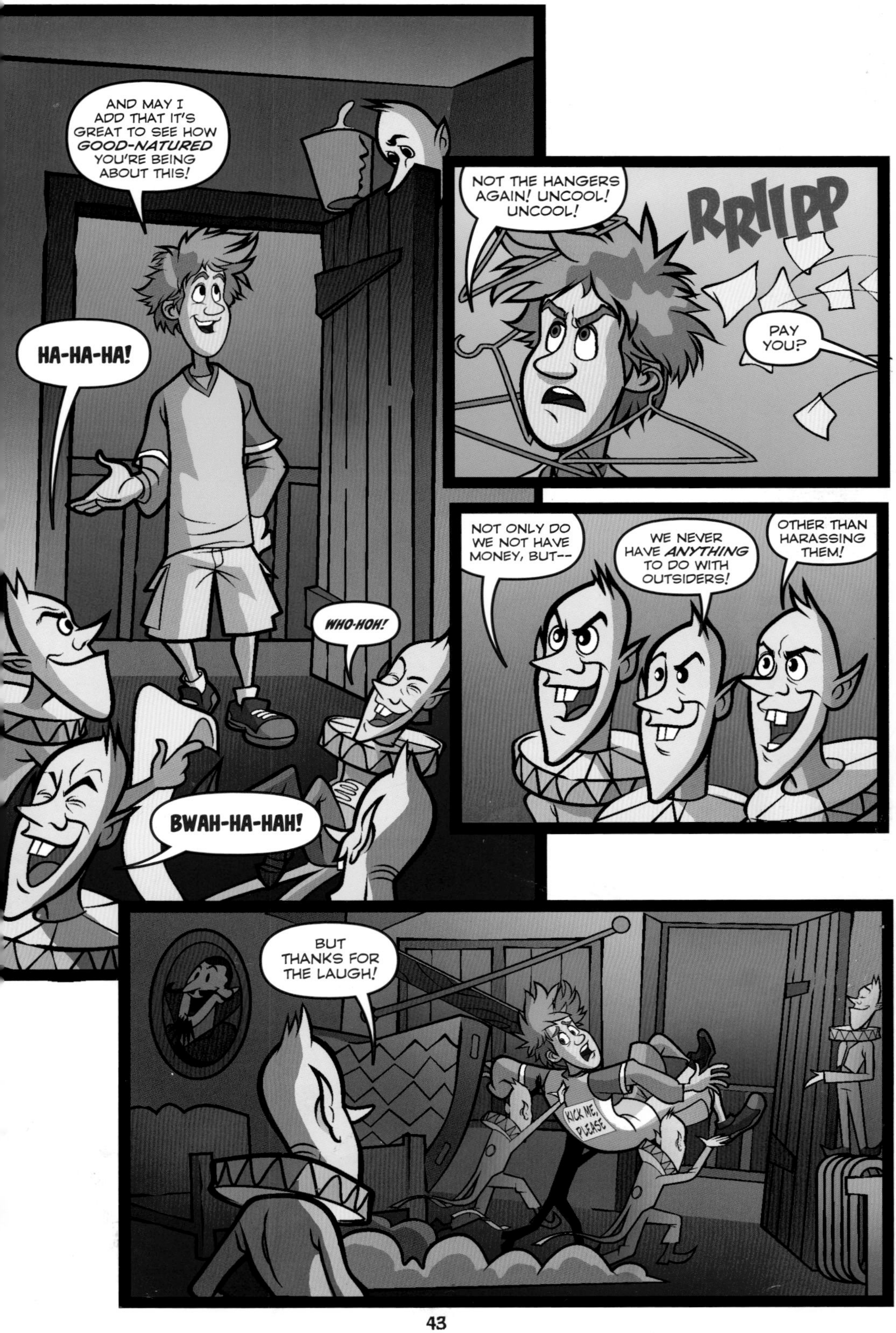
AND MAY I ADD THAT IT'S GREAT TO SEE HOW *GOOD-NATURED* YOU'RE BEING ABOUT THIS!
HA-HA-HA!
WHO-HOH!
BWAH-HA-HAH!
NOT THE HANGERS AGAIN! UNCOOL! UNCOOL!
RRIIPP
PAY YOU?
NOT ONLY DO WE NOT HAVE MONEY, BUT--
WE NEVER HAVE *ANYTHING* TO DO WITH OUTSIDERS!
OTHER THAN HARASSING THEM!
BUT THANKS FOR THE LAUGH!
KICK ME, PLEASE

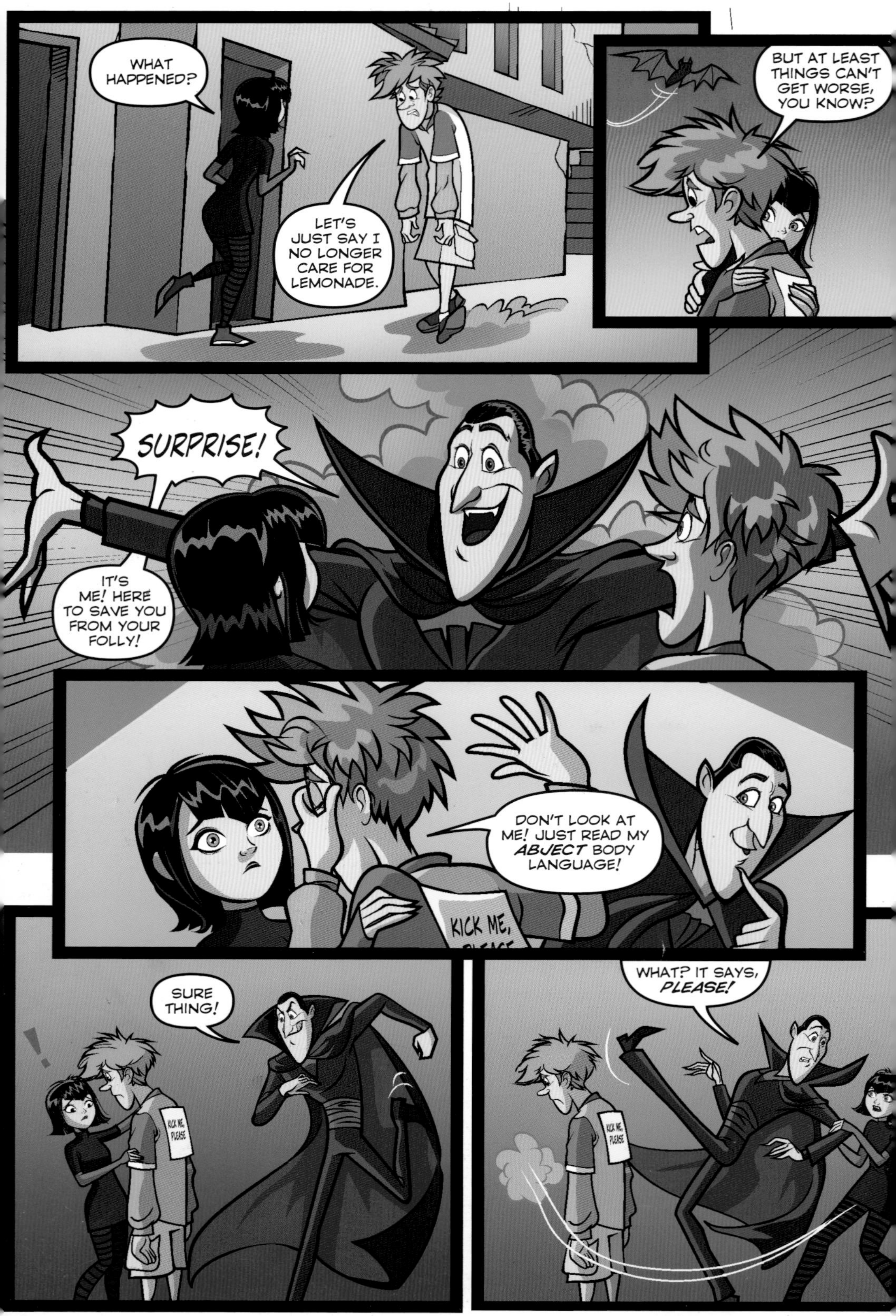
WHAT HAPPENED?
LET'S JUST SAY I NO LONGER CARE FOR LEMONADE.
BUT AT LEAST THINGS CAN'T GET WORSE, YOU KNOW?
SURPRISE!
IT'S ME! HERE TO SAVE YOU FROM YOUR FOLLY!
DON'T LOOK AT ME! JUST READ MY *ABJECT* BODY LANGUAGE!
KICK ME,
SURE THING!
!
KICK ME, PLEASE
WHAT? IT SAYS, *PLEASE!*
KICK ME, PLEASE

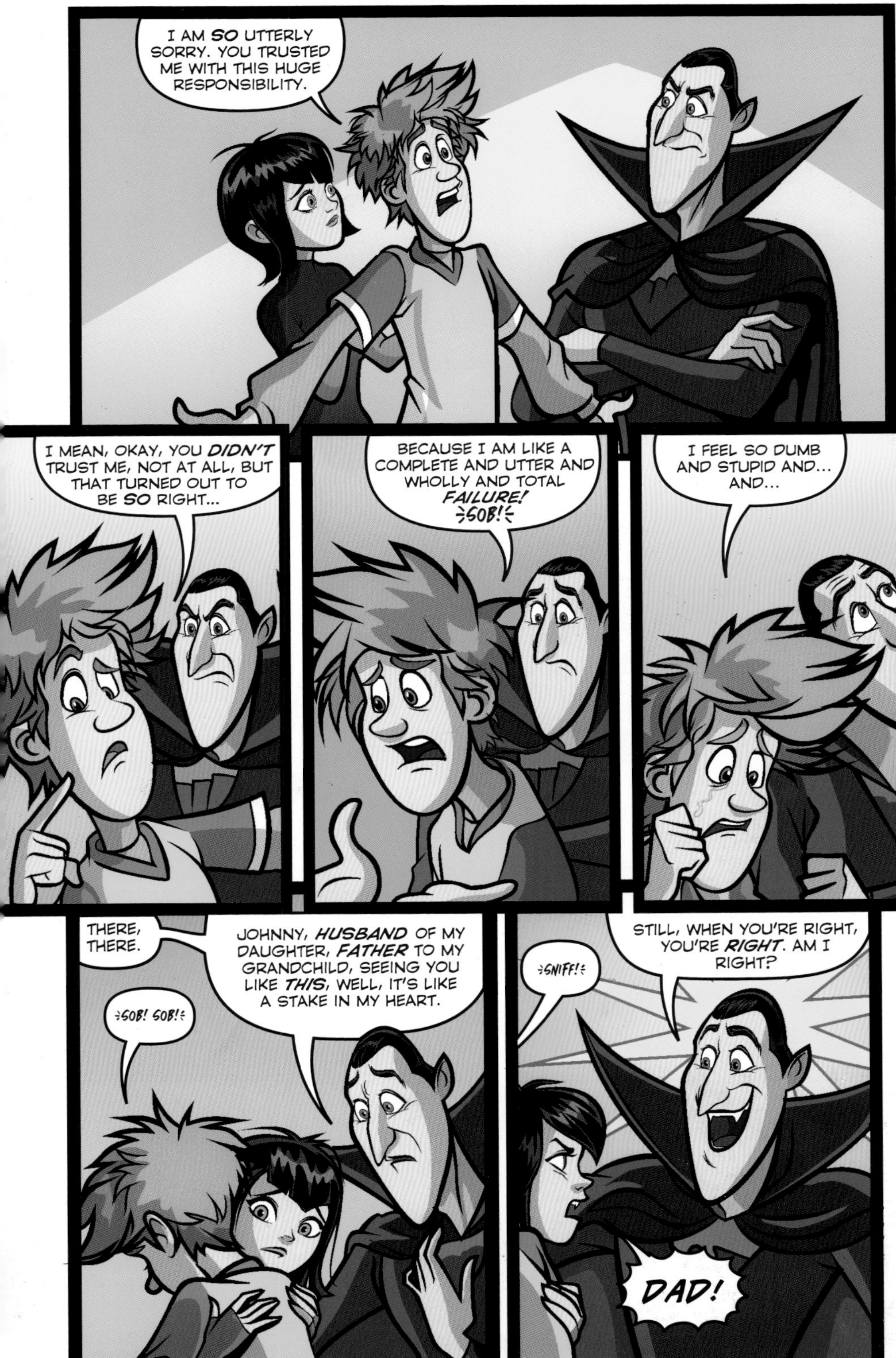
I AM SO UTTERLY SORRY. YOU TRUSTED ME WITH THIS HUGE RESPONSIBILITY.
I MEAN, OKAY, YOU DIDN'T TRUST ME, NOT AT ALL, BUT THAT TURNED OUT TO BE SO RIGHT...
BECAUSE I AM LIKE A COMPLETE AND UTTER AND WHOLLY AND TOTAL FAILURE!
SOB!
I FEEL SO DUMB AND STUPID AND... AND...
THERE, THERE.
SOB! SOB!
JOHNNY, HUSBAND OF MY DAUGHTER, FATHER TO MY GRANDCHILD, SEEING YOU LIKE THIS, WELL, IT'S LIKE A STAKE IN MY HEART.
SNIFF!
STILL, WHEN YOU'RE RIGHT, YOU'RE RIGHT. AM I RIGHT?
DAD!

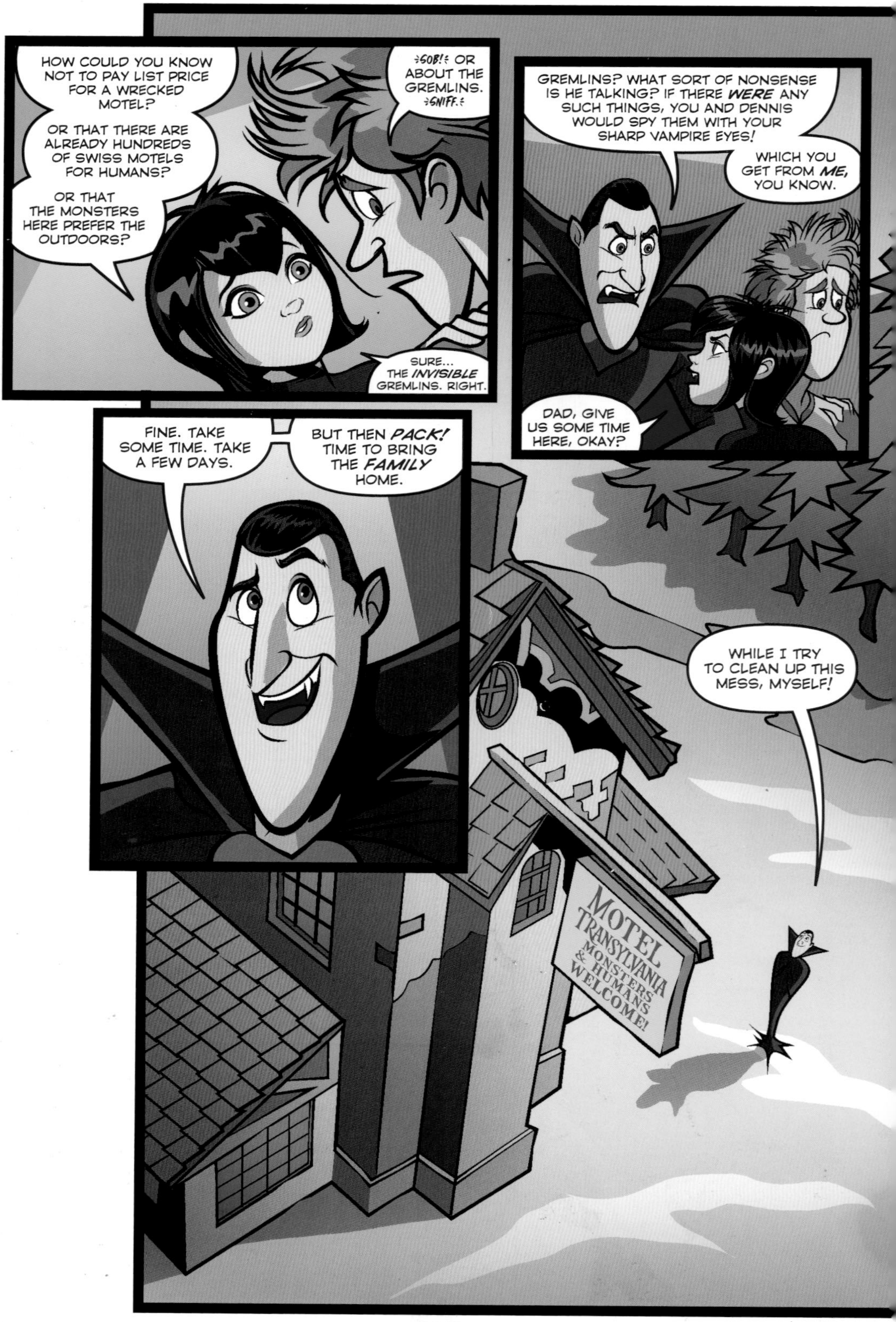
HOW COULD YOU KNOW NOT TO PAY LIST PRICE FOR A WRECKED MOTEL?
OR THAT THERE ARE ALREADY HUNDREDS OF SWISS MOTELS FOR HUMANS?
OR THAT THE MONSTERS HERE PREFER THE OUTDOORS?
SOB! OR ABOUT THE GREMLINS. *SNIFF.*
SURE... THE INVISIBLE GREMLINS. RIGHT.
GREMLINS? WHAT SORT OF NONSENSE IS HE TALKING? IF THERE WERE ANY SUCH THINGS, YOU AND DENNIS WOULD SPY THEM WITH YOUR SHARP VAMPIRE EYES!
WHICH YOU GET FROM ME, YOU KNOW.
DAD, GIVE US SOME TIME HERE, OKAY?
FINE. TAKE SOME TIME. TAKE A FEW DAYS.
BUT THEN PACK! TIME TO BRING THE FAMILY HOME.
WHILE I TRY TO CLEAN UP THIS MESS, MYSELF!
MOTEL TRANSYLVANIA MONSTERS & HUMANS WELCOME!

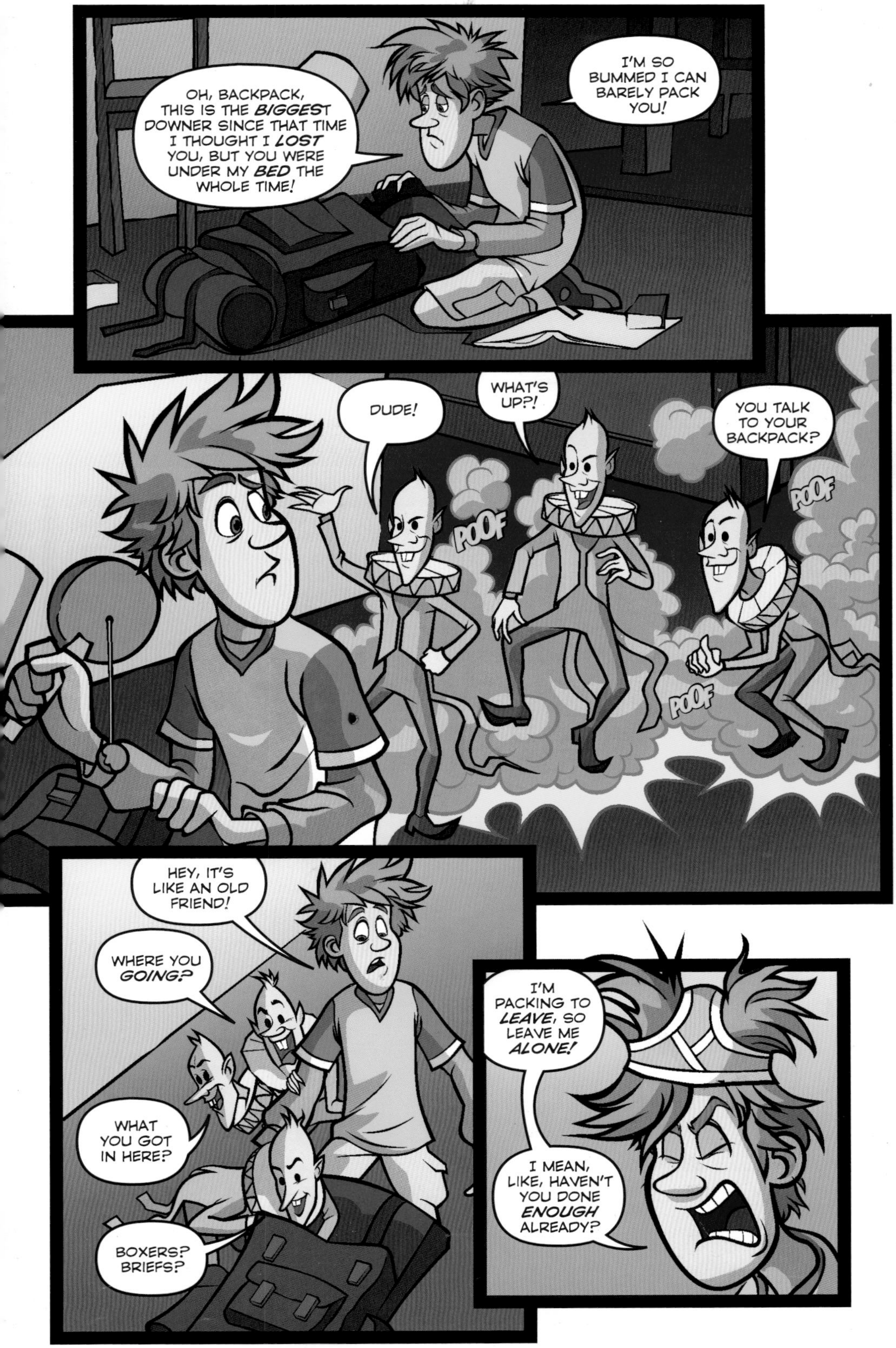
OH, BACKPACK, THIS IS THE *BIGGEST* DOWNER SINCE THAT TIME I THOUGHT I *LOST* YOU, BUT YOU WERE UNDER MY *BED* THE WHOLE TIME!
I'M SO BUMMED I CAN BARELY PACK YOU!
DUDE!
WHAT'S UP?!
YOU TALK TO YOUR BACKPACK?
POOF
POOF
POOF
HEY, IT'S LIKE AN OLD FRIEND!
WHERE YOU *GOING?*
WHAT YOU GOT IN HERE?
BOXERS? BRIEFS?
I'M PACKING TO *LEAVE*, SO LEAVE ME *ALONE!*
I MEAN, LIKE, HAVEN'T YOU DONE *ENOUGH* ALREADY?

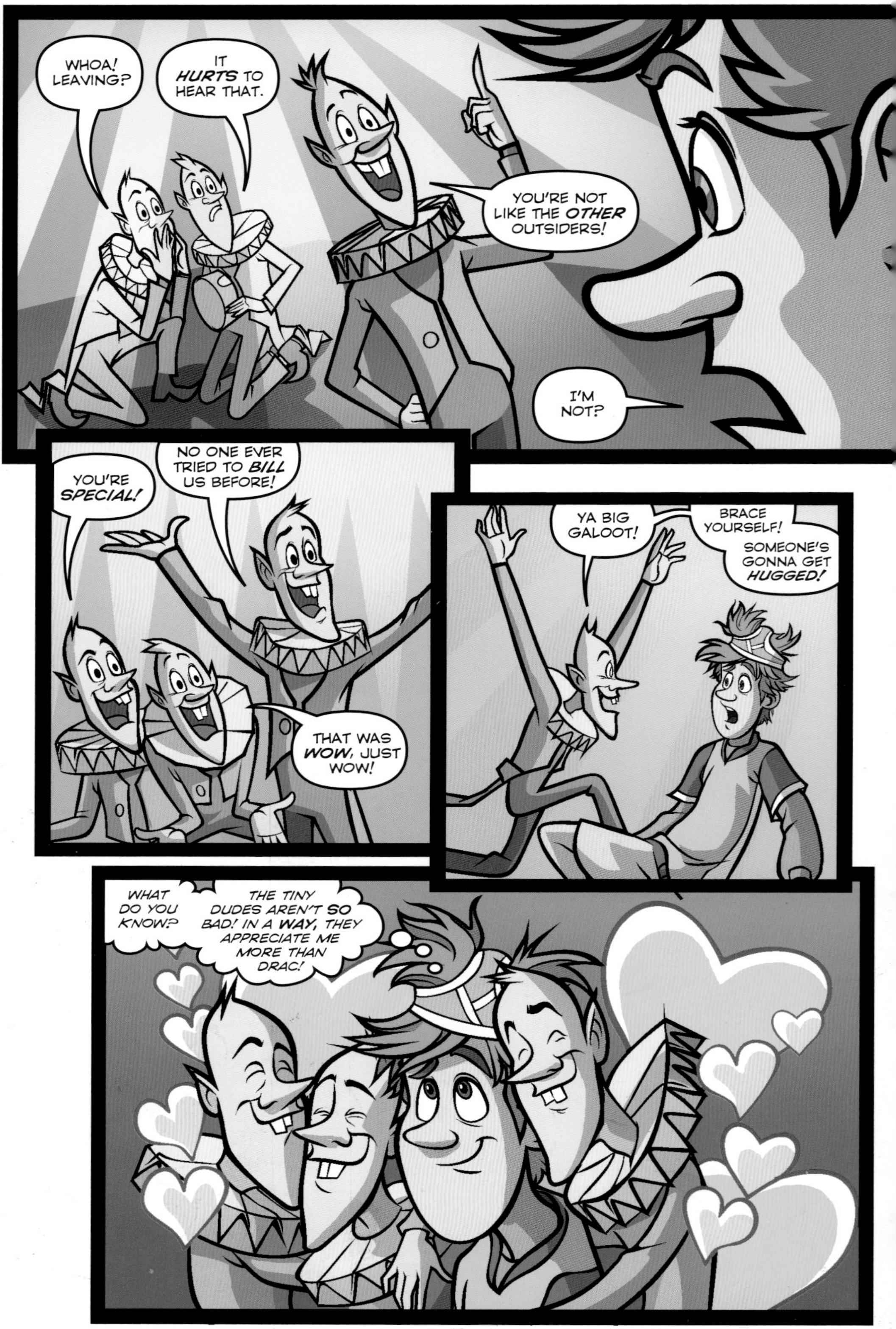
WHOA! LEAVING?
IT HURTS TO HEAR THAT.
YOU'RE NOT LIKE THE OTHER OUTSIDERS!
I'M NOT?
YOU'RE SPECIAL!
NO ONE EVER TRIED TO BILL US BEFORE!
THAT WAS WOW, JUST WOW!
YA BIG GALOOT!
BRACE YOURSELF!
SOMEONE'S GONNA GET HUGGED!
WHAT DO YOU KNOW?
THE TINY DUDES AREN'T SO BAD! IN A WAY, THEY APPRECIATE ME MORE THAN DRAC!

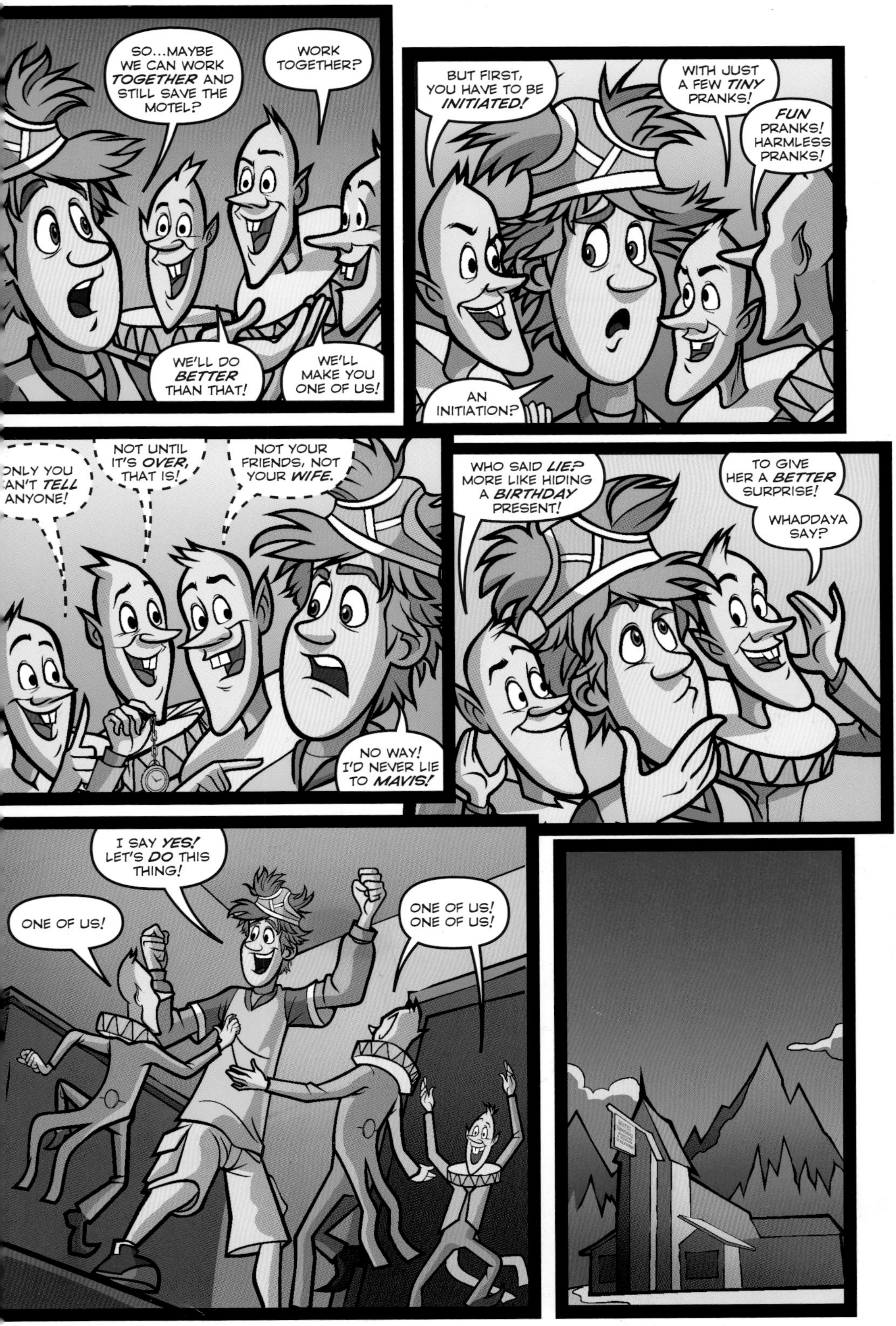
SO...MAYBE WE CAN WORK TOGETHER AND STILL SAVE THE MOTEL?
WORK TOGETHER?
WE'LL DO BETTER THAN THAT!
WE'LL MAKE YOU ONE OF US!
BUT FIRST, YOU HAVE TO BE INITIATED!
WITH JUST A FEW TINY PRANKS!
FUN PRANKS! HARMLESS PRANKS!
AN INITIATION?
ONLY YOU CAN'T TELL ANYONE!
NOT UNTIL IT'S OVER, THAT IS!
NOT YOUR FRIENDS, NOT YOUR WIFE.
NO WAY! I'D NEVER LIE TO MAVIS!
WHO SAID LIE? MORE LIKE HIDING A BIRTHDAY PRESENT!
TO GIVE HER A BETTER SURPRISE!
WHADDAYA SAY?
I SAY YES! LET'S DO THIS THING!
ONE OF US!
ONE OF US! ONE OF US!

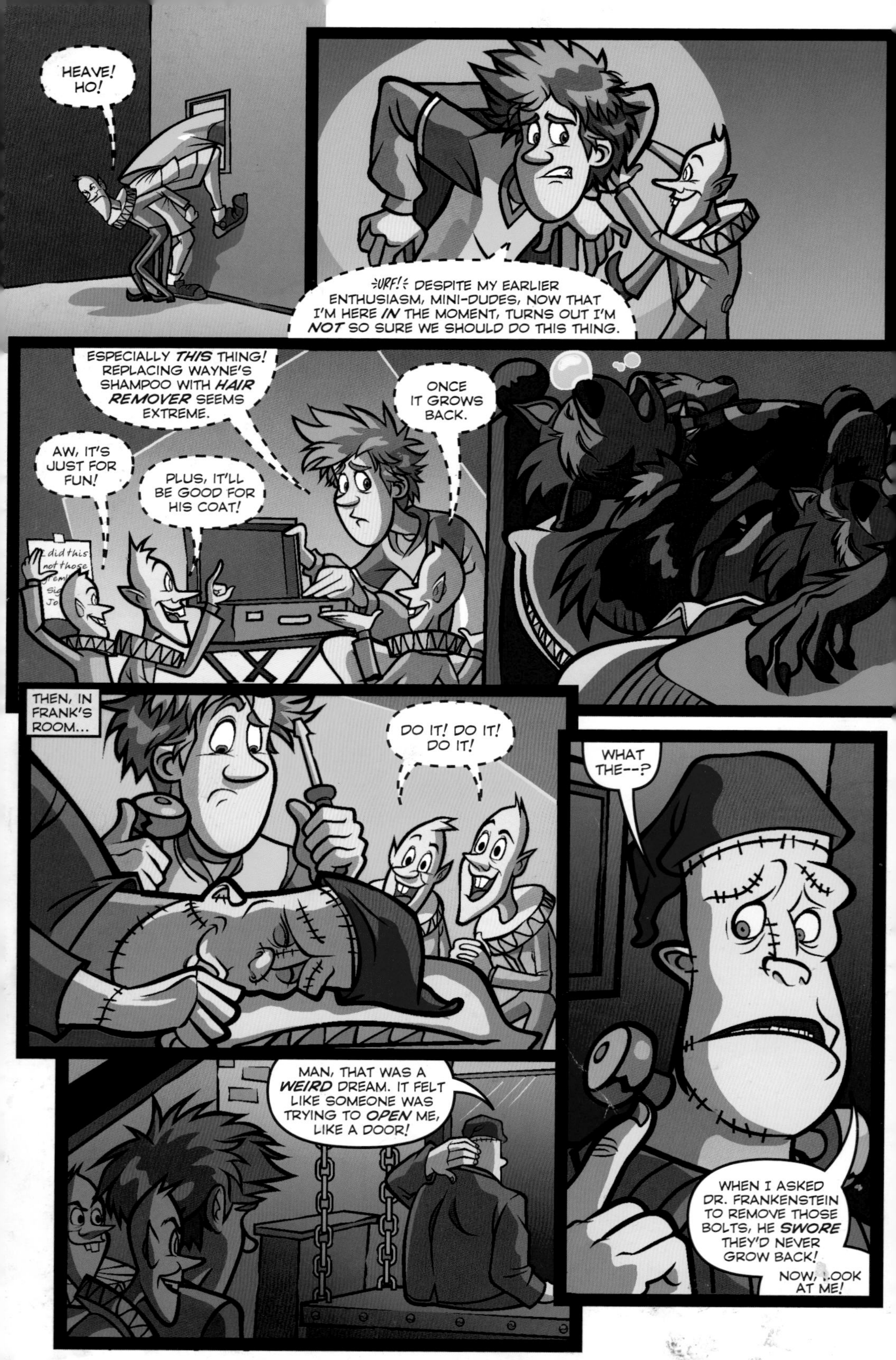
HEAVE! HO!
URF! DESPITE MY EARLIER ENTHUSIASM, MINI-DUDES, NOW THAT I'M HERE *IN* THE MOMENT, TURNS OUT I'M *NOT* SO SURE WE SHOULD DO THIS THING.
ESPECIALLY *THIS* THING! REPLACING WAYNE'S SHAMPOO WITH *HAIR REMOVER* SEEMS EXTREME.
AW, IT'S JUST FOR FUN!
PLUS, IT'LL BE GOOD FOR HIS COAT!
ONCE IT GROWS BACK.
THEN, IN FRANK'S ROOM...
DO IT! DO IT! DO IT!
WHAT THE--?
WHEN I ASKED DR. FRANKENSTEIN TO REMOVE THOSE BOLTS, HE *SWORE* THEY'D NEVER GROW BACK!
NOW, LOOK AT ME!
MAN, THAT WAS A *WEIRD* DREAM. IT FELT LIKE SOMEONE WAS TRYING TO *OPEN* ME, LIKE A DOOR!

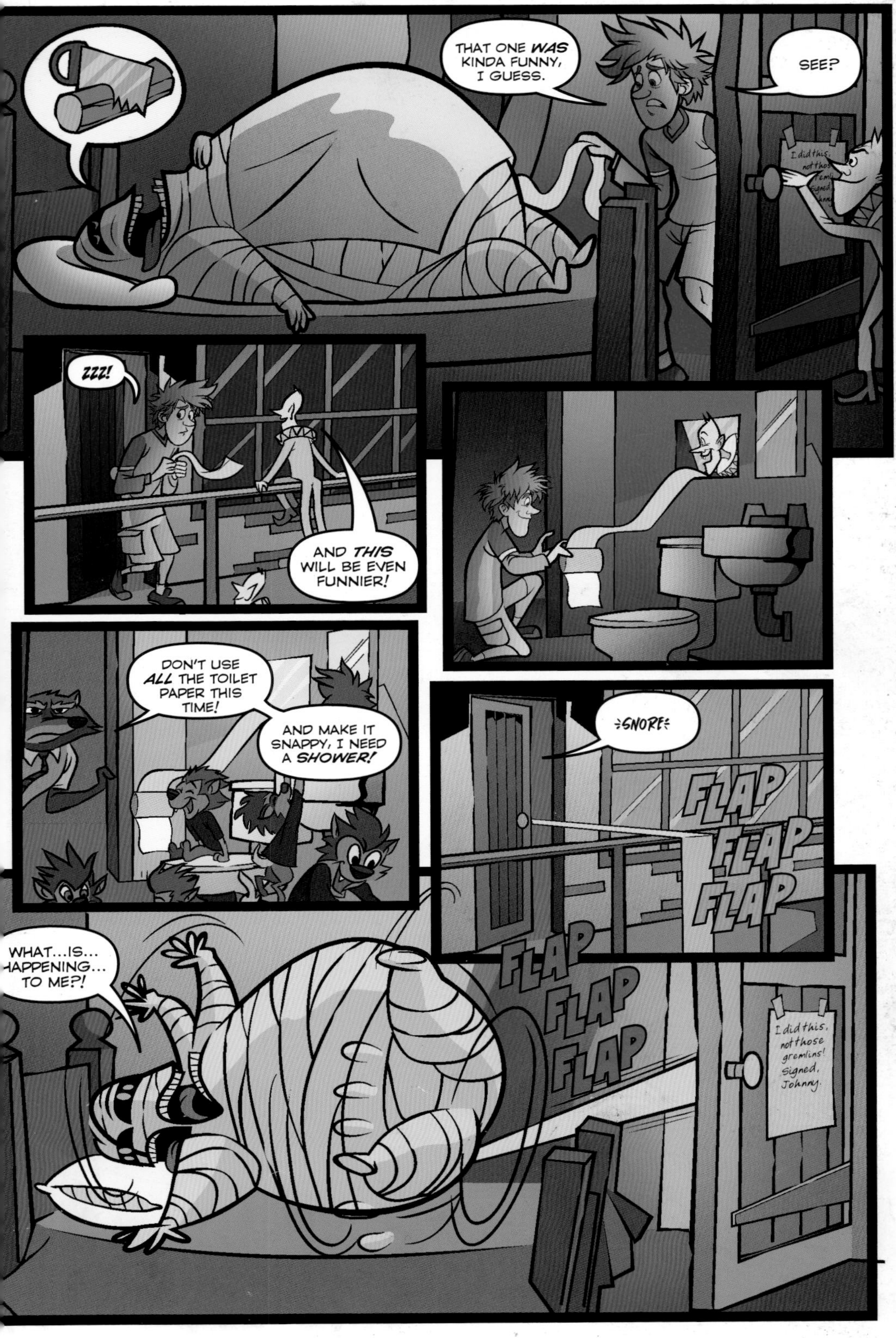
THAT ONE *WAS* KINDA FUNNY, I GUESS.
SEE?
ZZZ!
AND *THIS* WILL BE EVEN FUNNIER!
DON'T USE *ALL* THE TOILET PAPER THIS TIME!
AND MAKE IT SNAPPY, I NEED A *SHOWER!*
SNORE
FLAP
FLAP
FLAP
WHAT...IS... HAPPENING... TO ME?!
FLAP
FLAP
FLAP
I did this, not those gremlins! Signed, Johnny.

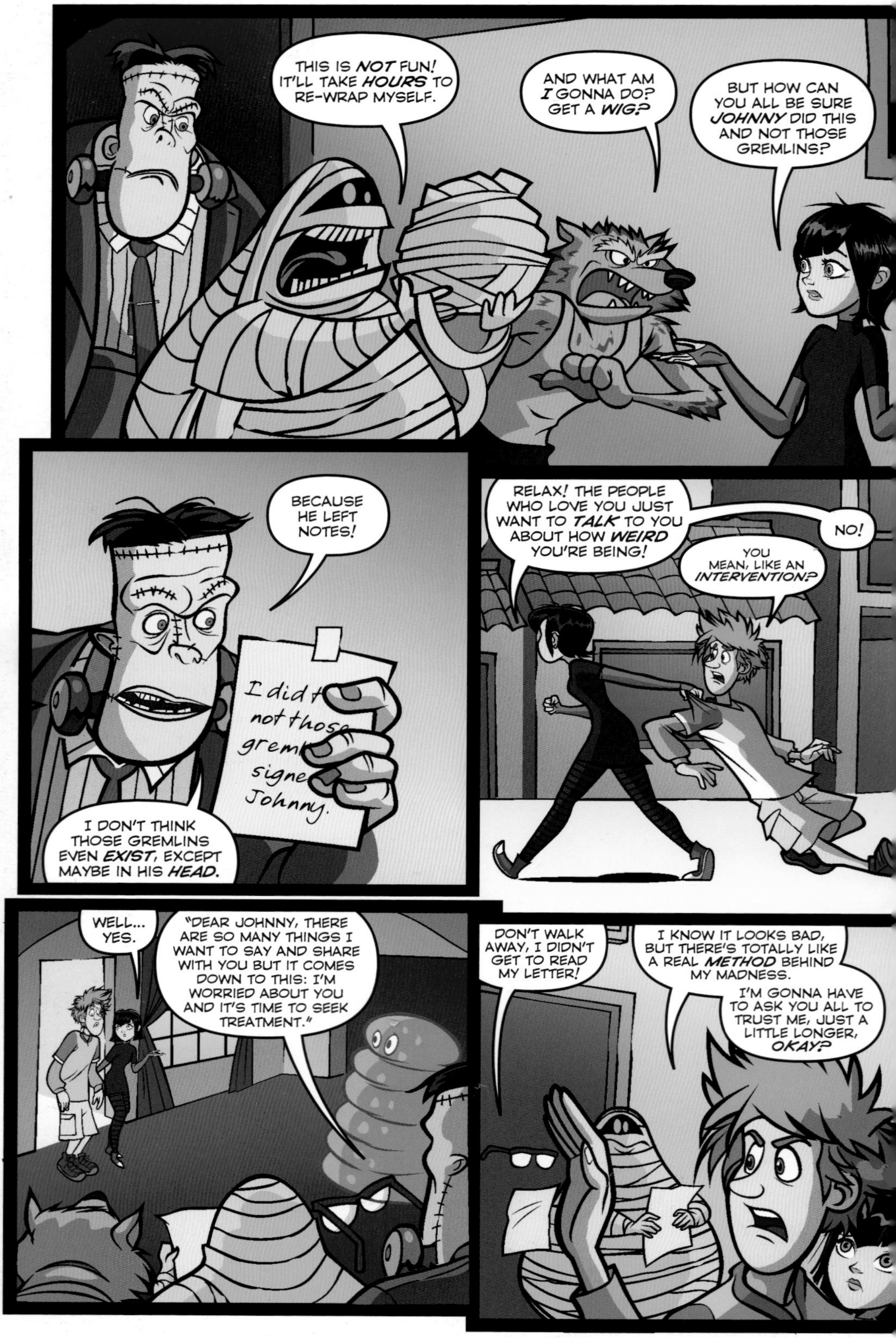
THIS IS NOT FUN! IT'LL TAKE HOURS TO RE-WRAP MYSELF.
AND WHAT AM I GONNA DO? GET A WIG?
BUT HOW CAN YOU ALL BE SURE JOHNNY DID THIS AND NOT THOSE GREMLINS?
BECAUSE HE LEFT NOTES!
Johnny.
I DON'T THINK THOSE GREMLINS EVEN EXIST, EXCEPT MAYBE IN HIS HEAD.
RELAX! THE PEOPLE WHO LOVE YOU JUST WANT TO TALK TO YOU ABOUT HOW WEIRD YOU'RE BEING!
NO!
YOU MEAN, LIKE AN INTERVENTION?
WELL... YES.
"DEAR JOHNNY, THERE ARE SO MANY THINGS I WANT TO SAY AND SHARE WITH YOU BUT IT COMES DOWN TO THIS: I'M WORRIED ABOUT YOU AND IT'S TIME TO SEEK TREATMENT."
DON'T WALK AWAY, I DIDN'T GET TO READ MY LETTER!
I KNOW IT LOOKS BAD, BUT THERE'S TOTALLY LIKE A REAL METHOD BEHIND MY MADNESS.
I'M GONNA HAVE TO ASK YOU ALL TO TRUST ME, JUST A LITTLE LONGER, OKAY?

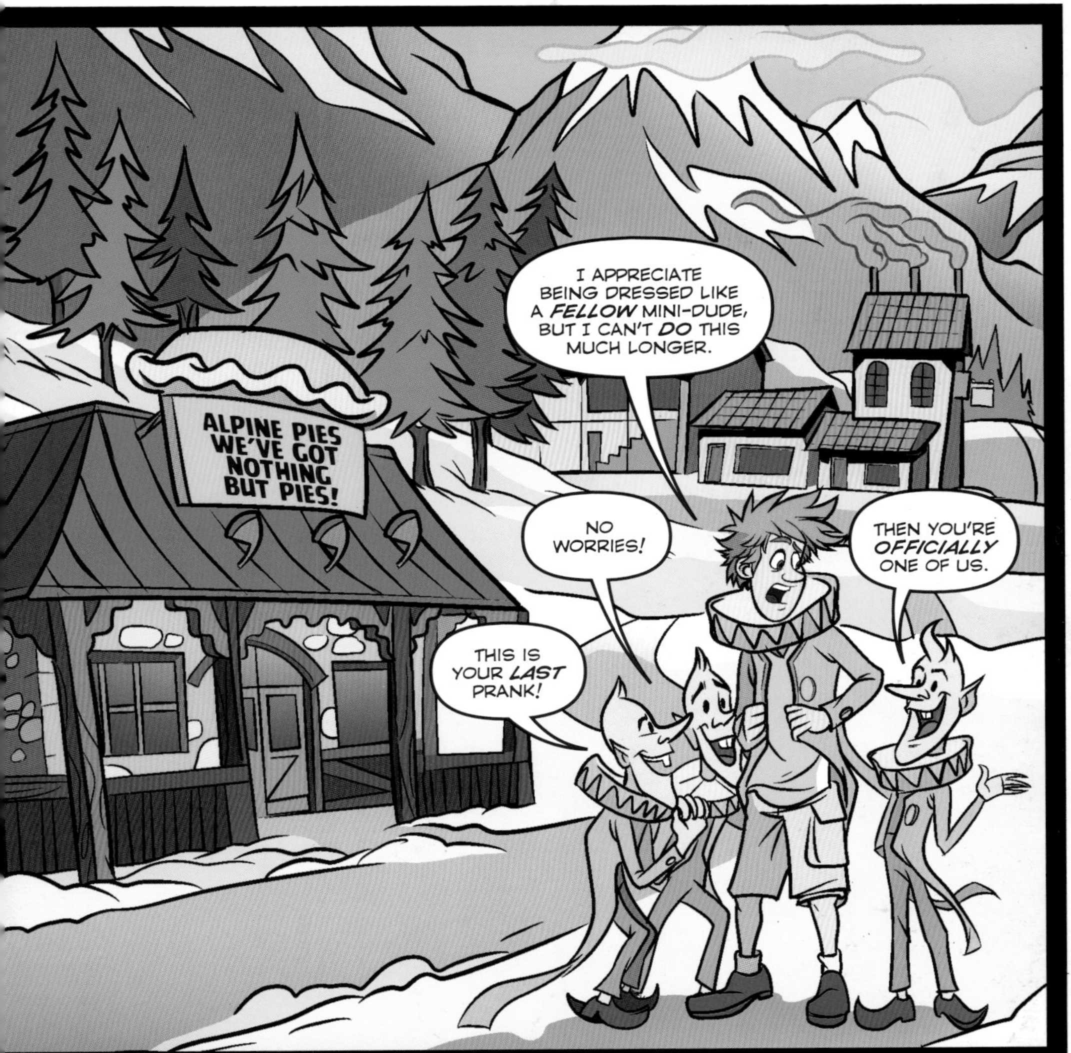
ALPINE PIES WE'VE GOT NOTHING BUT PIES!
I APPRECIATE BEING DRESSED LIKE A *FELLOW* MINI-DUDE, BUT I CAN'T *DO* THIS MUCH LONGER.
NO WORRIES!
THEN YOU'RE *OFFICIALLY* ONE OF US.
THIS IS YOUR *LAST* PRANK!

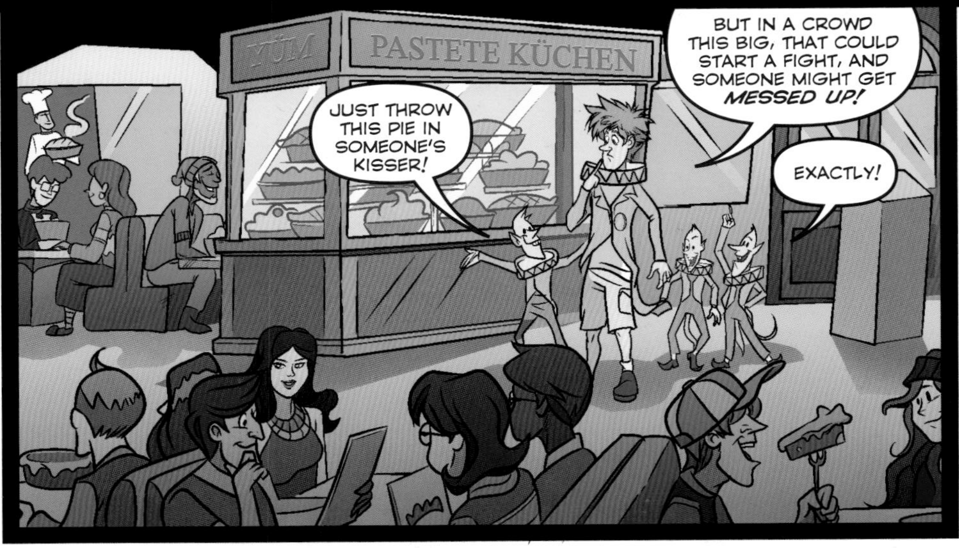
YÜM
PASTETE KÜCHEN
JUST THROW THIS PIE IN SOMEONE'S KISSER!
BUT IN A CROWD THIS BIG, THAT COULD START A FIGHT, AND SOMEONE MIGHT GET ***MESSED UP!***
EXACTLY!

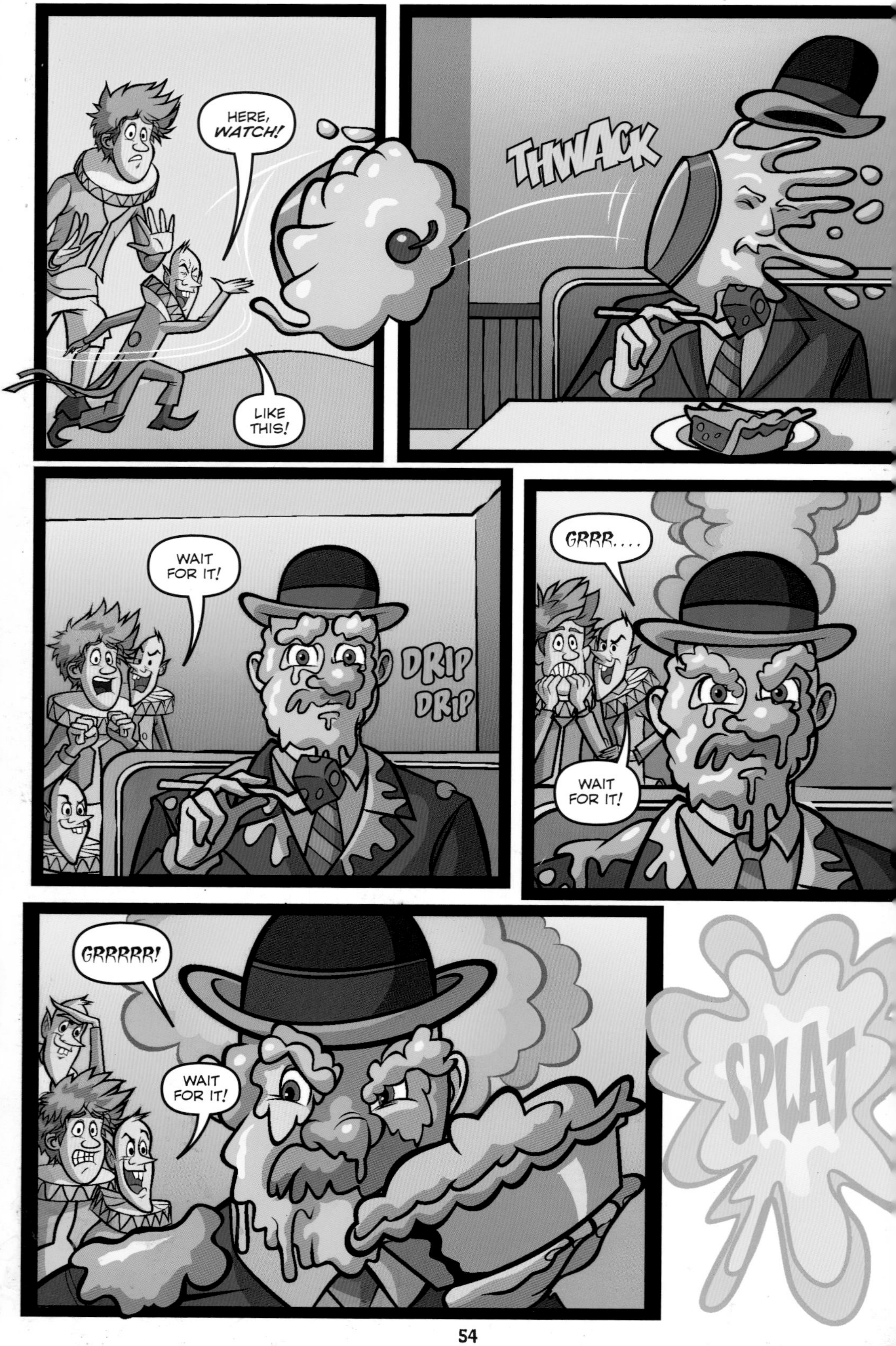
HERE, WATCH!
LIKE THIS!
THWACK
WAIT FOR IT!
DRIP
DRIP
GRRR....
WAIT FOR IT!
GRRRRR!
WAIT FOR IT!
SPLAT

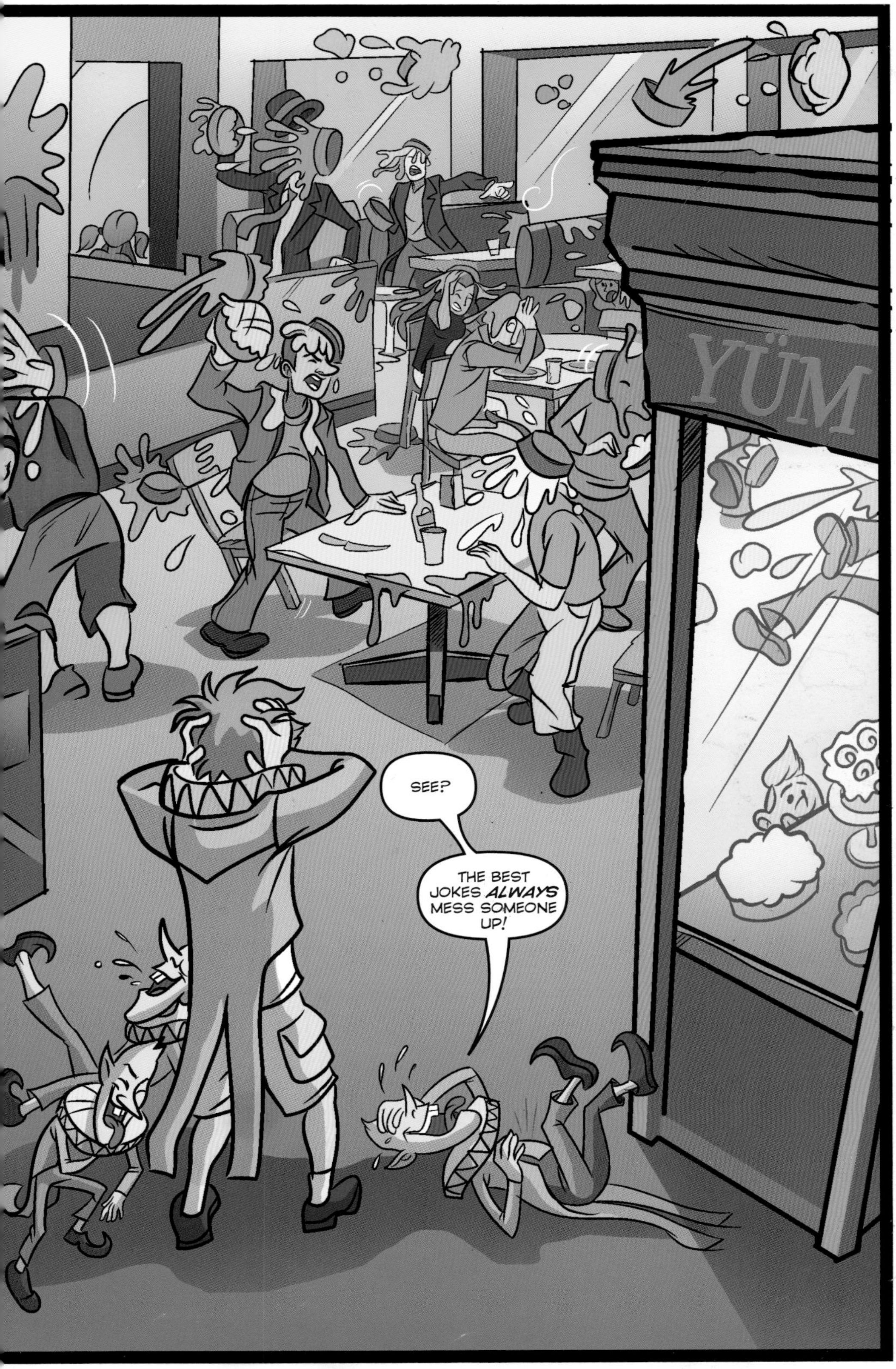
YÜM
SEE?
THE BEST JOKES *ALWAYS* MESS SOMEONE UP!

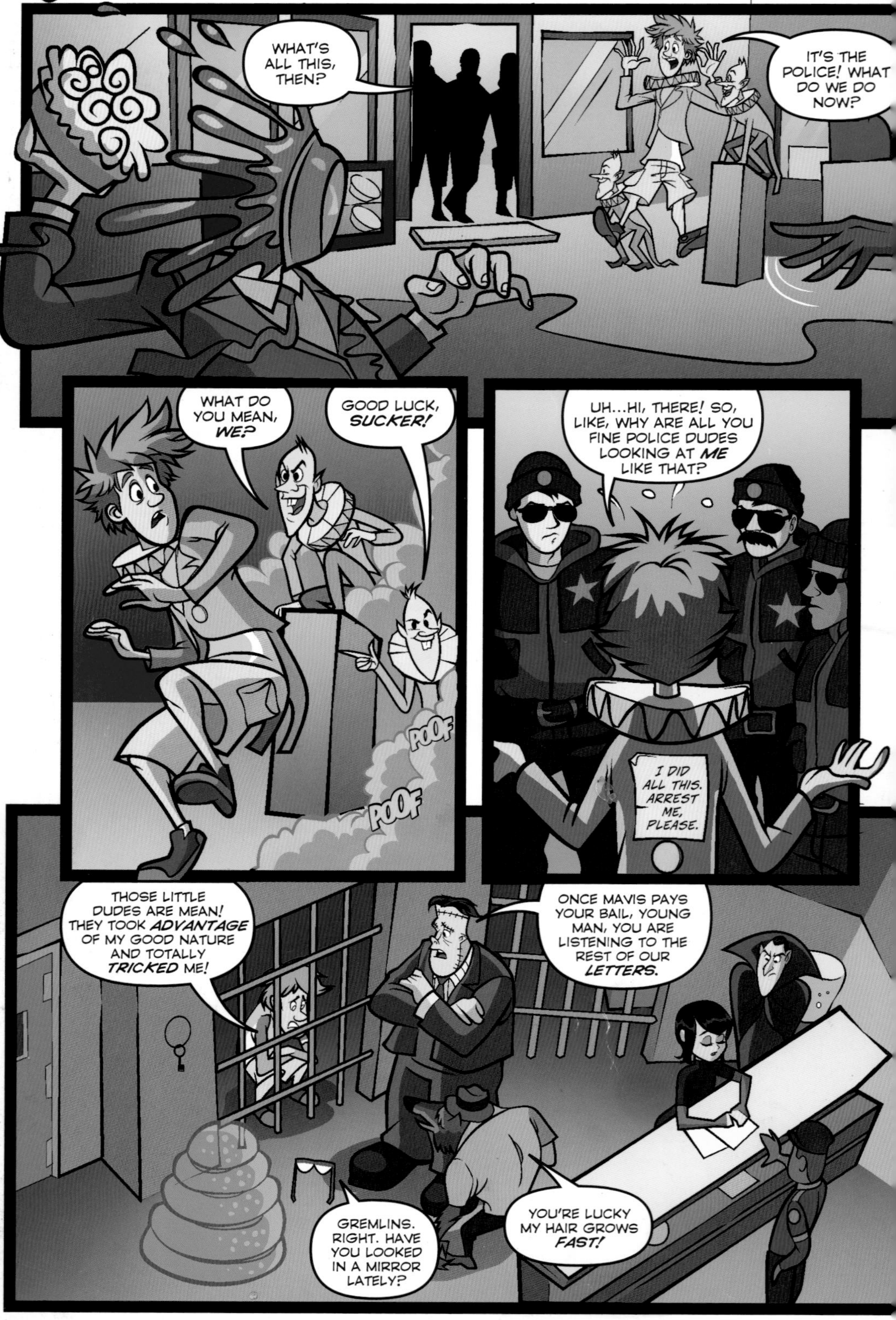
WHAT'S ALL THIS, THEN?
IT'S THE POLICE! WHAT DO WE DO NOW?
WHAT DO YOU MEAN, WE?
GOOD LUCK, SUCKER!
POOF
POOF
UH...HI, THERE! SO, LIKE, WHY ARE ALL YOU FINE POLICE DUDES LOOKING AT ME LIKE THAT?
I DID ALL THIS. ARREST ME, PLEASE.
THOSE LITTLE DUDES ARE MEAN! THEY TOOK ADVANTAGE OF MY GOOD NATURE AND TOTALLY TRICKED ME!
ONCE MAVIS PAYS YOUR BAIL, YOUNG MAN, YOU ARE LISTENING TO THE REST OF OUR LETTERS.
GREMLINS. RIGHT. HAVE YOU LOOKED IN A MIRROR LATELY?
YOU'RE LUCKY MY HAIR GROWS FAST!

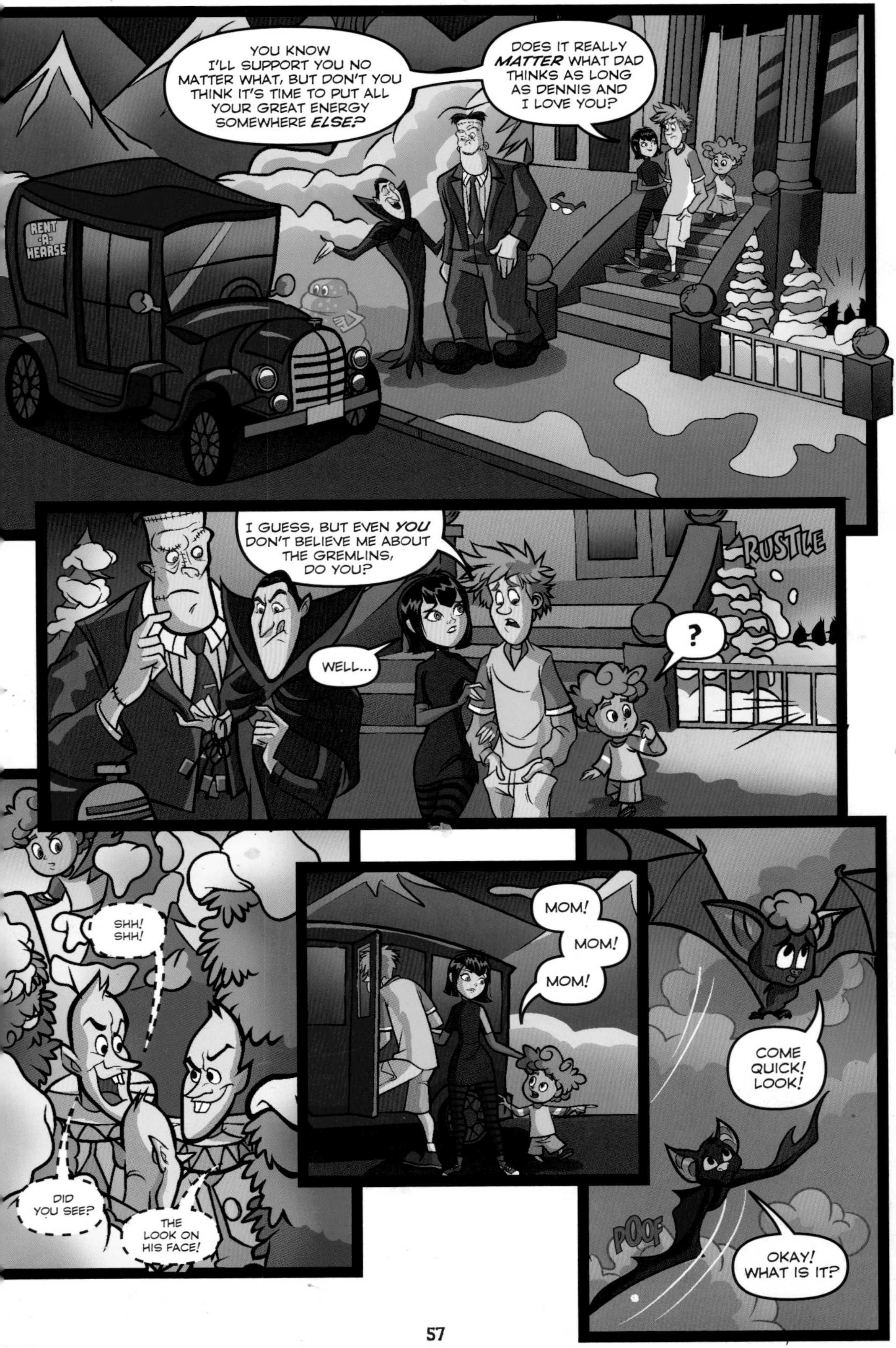
YOU KNOW I'LL SUPPORT YOU NO MATTER WHAT, BUT DON'T YOU THINK IT'S TIME TO PUT ALL YOUR GREAT ENERGY SOMEWHERE *ELSE?*
DOES IT REALLY *MATTER* WHAT DAD THINKS AS LONG AS DENNIS AND I LOVE YOU?
RENT -A- HEARSE
I GUESS, BUT EVEN *YOU* DON'T BELIEVE ME ABOUT THE GREMLINS, DO YOU?
WELL...
RUSTLE
?
SHH! SHH!
DID YOU SEE?
THE LOOK ON HIS FACE!
MOM!
MOM!
MOM!
COME QUICK! LOOK!
POOF
OKAY! WHAT IS IT?

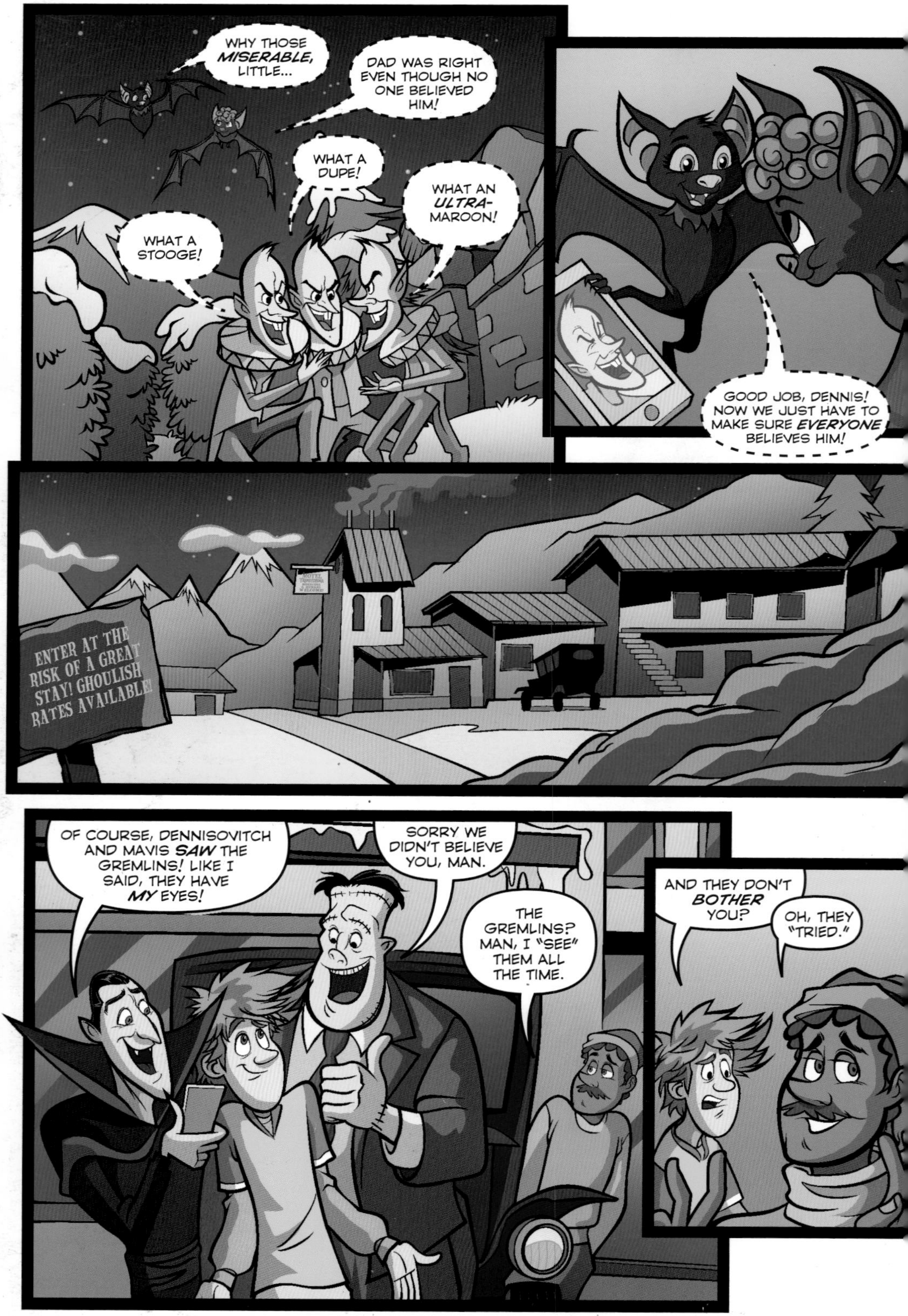
WHY THOSE **MISERABLE,** LITTLE...
DAD WAS RIGHT EVEN THOUGH NO ONE BELIEVED HIM!
WHAT A DUPE!
WHAT AN **ULTRA-**MAROON!
WHAT A STOOGE!
GOOD JOB, DENNIS! NOW WE JUST HAVE TO MAKE SURE **EVERYONE** BELIEVES HIM!
ENTER AT THE RISK OF A GREAT STAY! GHOULISH RATES AVAILABLE!
OF COURSE, DENNISOVITCH AND MAVIS **SAW** THE GREMLINS! LIKE I SAID, THEY HAVE **MY** EYES!
SORRY WE DIDN'T BELIEVE YOU, MAN.
THE GREMLINS? MAN, I "SEE" THEM ALL THE TIME.
AND THEY DON'T **BOTHER** YOU?
OH, THEY "TRIED."

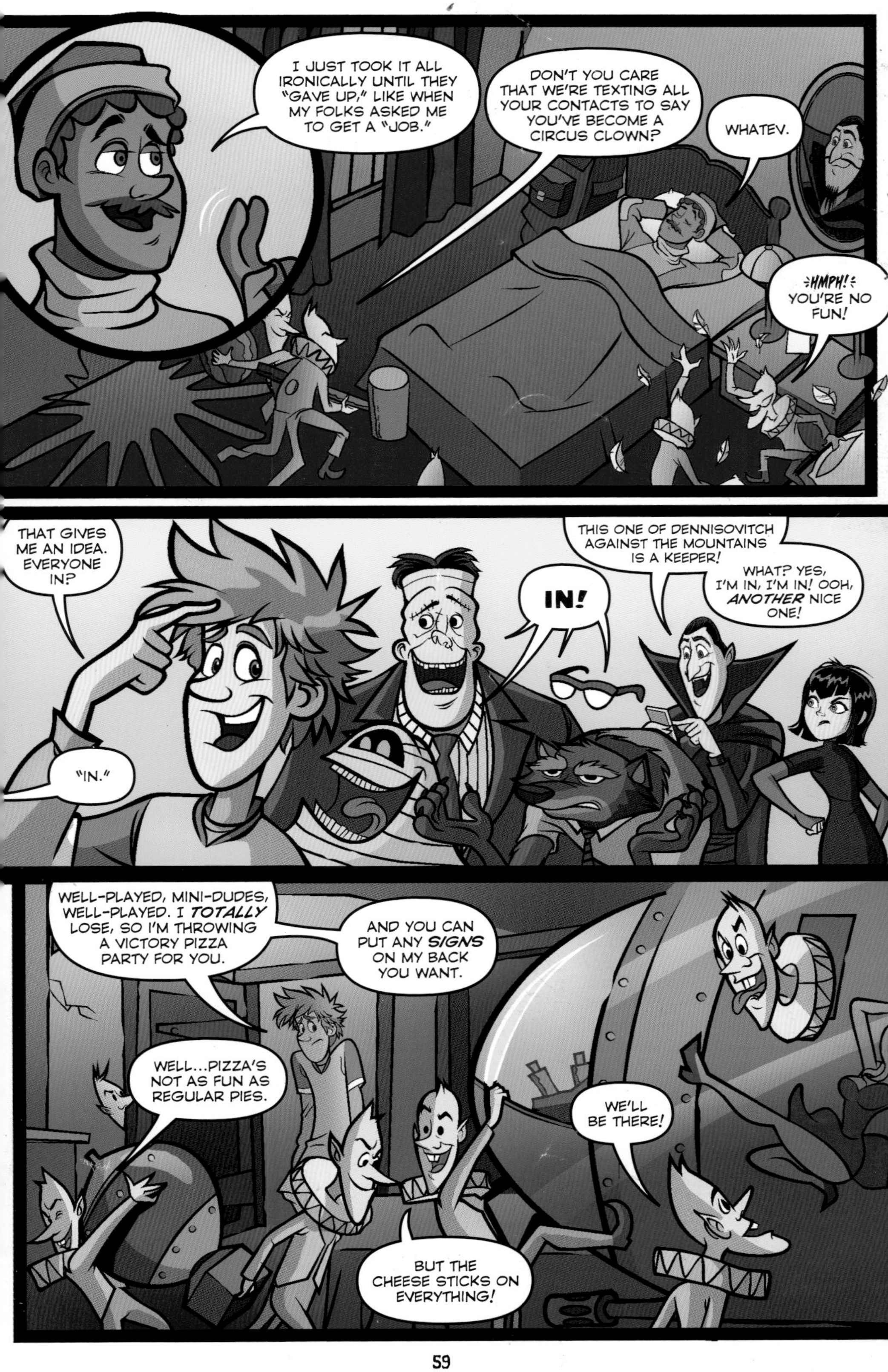

I JUST TOOK IT ALL IRONICALLY UNTIL THEY "GAVE UP," LIKE WHEN MY FOLKS ASKED ME TO GET A "JOB."
DON'T YOU CARE THAT WE'RE TEXTING ALL YOUR CONTACTS TO SAY YOU'VE BECOME A CIRCUS CLOWN?
WHATEV.
HMPH! YOU'RE NO FUN!
THAT GIVES ME AN IDEA. EVERYONE IN?
"IN."
IN!
THIS ONE OF DENNISOVITCH AGAINST THE MOUNTAINS IS A KEEPER!
WHAT? YES, I'M IN, I'M IN! OOH, ANOTHER NICE ONE!
WELL-PLAYED, MINI-DUDES, WELL-PLAYED. I TOTALLY LOSE, SO I'M THROWING A VICTORY PIZZA PARTY FOR YOU.
AND YOU CAN PUT ANY SIGNS ON MY BACK YOU WANT.
WELL...PIZZA'S NOT AS FUN AS REGULAR PIES.
WE'LL BE THERE!
BUT THE CHEESE STICKS ON EVERYTHING!

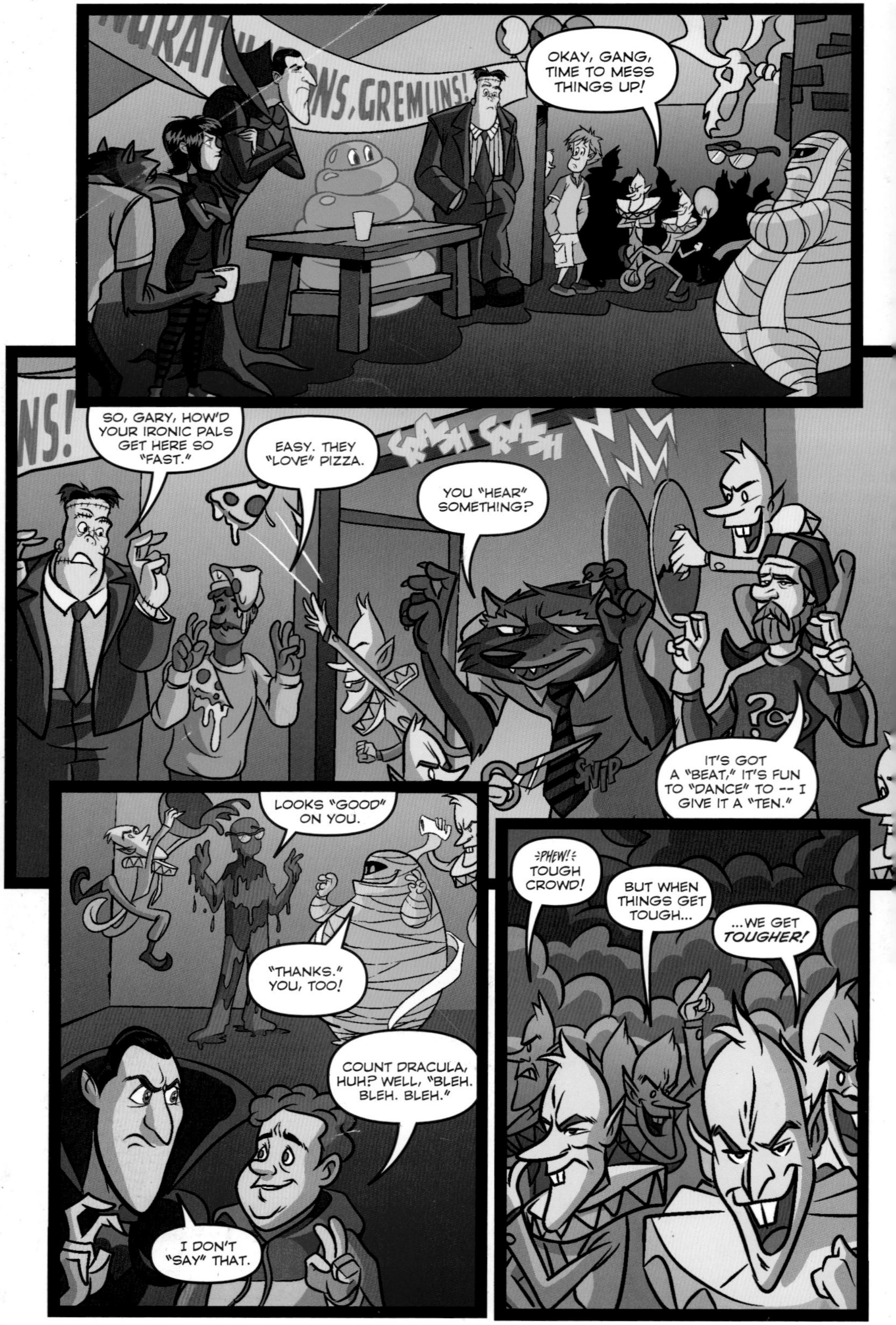
...NGRATU...NS, GREMLINS!
OKAY, GANG, TIME TO MESS THINGS UP!
...NS!
SO, GARY, HOW'D YOUR IRONIC PALS GET HERE SO "FAST."
EASY. THEY "LOVE" PIZZA.
CRASH CRASH
YOU "HEAR" SOMETHING?
SNIP
IT'S GOT A "BEAT," IT'S FUN TO "DANCE" TO -- I GIVE IT A "TEN."
LOOKS "GOOD" ON YOU.
"THANKS." YOU, TOO!
COUNT DRACULA, HUH? WELL, "BLEH. BLEH. BLEH."
I DON'T "SAY" THAT.
PHEW! TOUGH CROWD!
BUT WHEN THINGS GET TOUGH...
...WE GET TOUGHER!

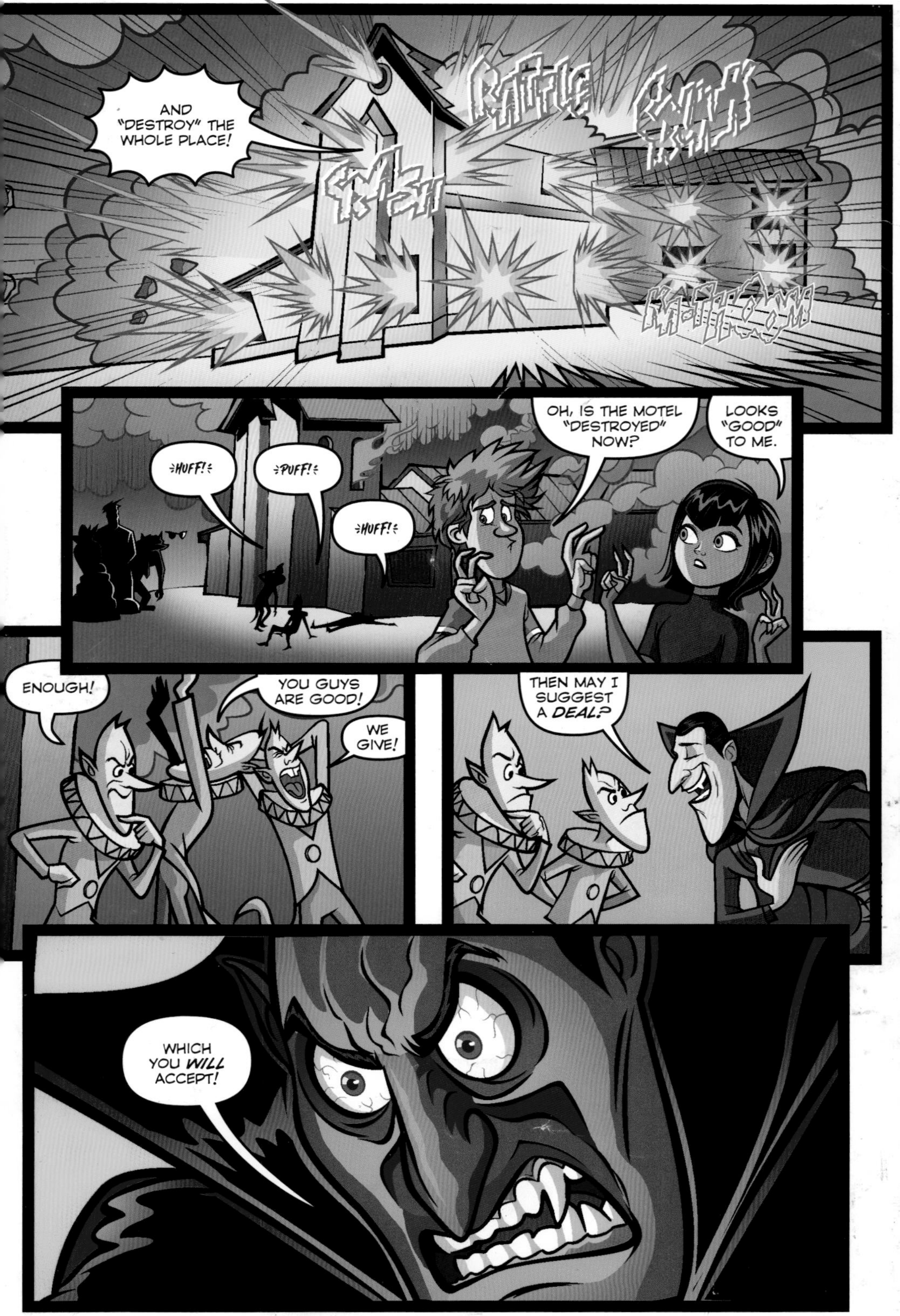
AND "DESTROY" THE WHOLE PLACE!
RATTLE
HUFF!
PUFF!
HUFF!
OH, IS THE MOTEL "DESTROYED" NOW?
LOOKS "GOOD" TO ME.
ENOUGH!
YOU GUYS ARE GOOD!
WE GIVE!
THEN MAY I SUGGEST A *DEAL?*
WHICH YOU *WILL* ACCEPT!

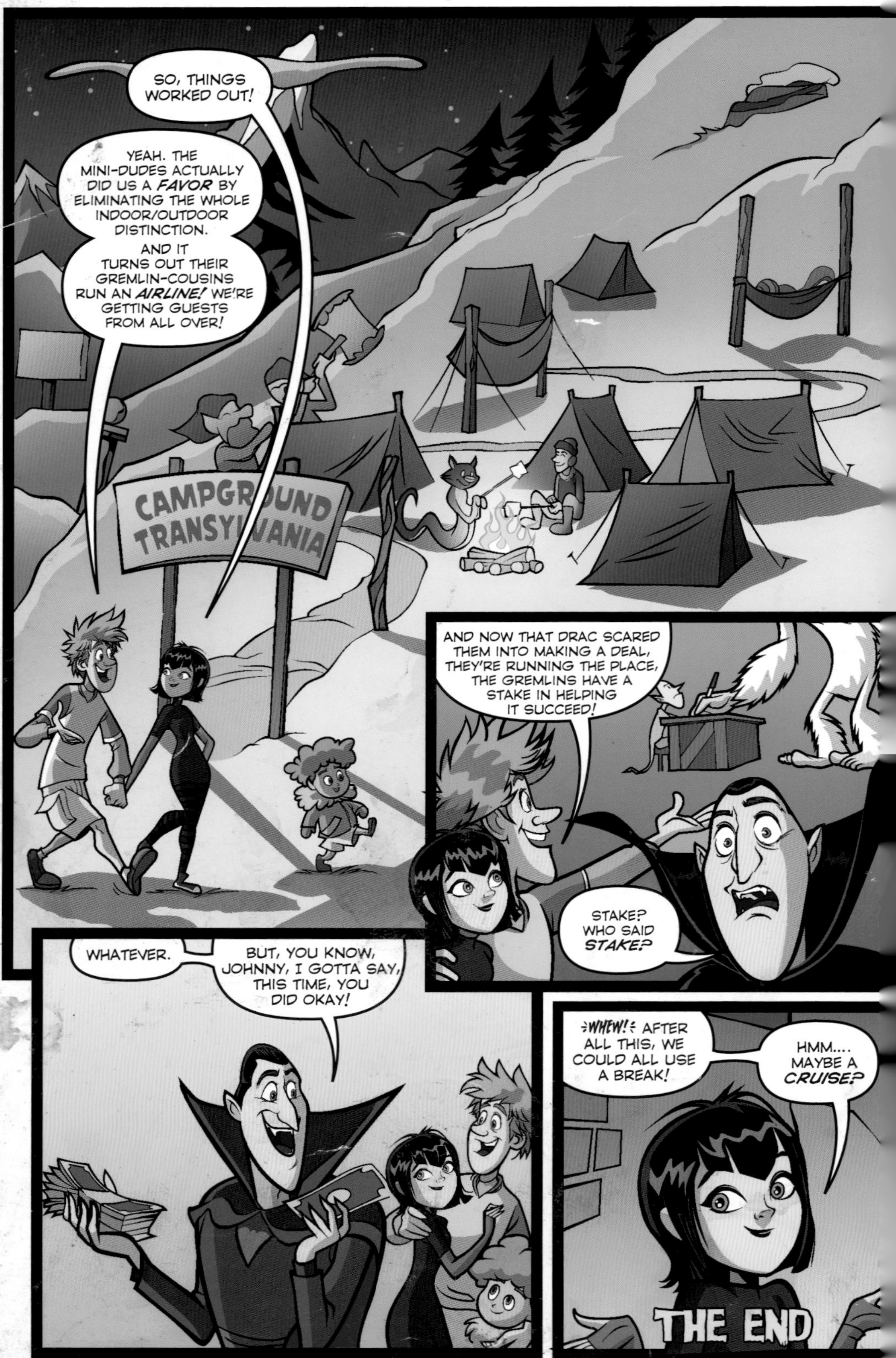
SO, THINGS WORKED OUT!
YEAH. THE MINI-DUDES ACTUALLY DID US A FAVOR BY ELIMINATING THE WHOLE INDOOR/OUTDOOR DISTINCTION.
AND IT TURNS OUT THEIR GREMLIN-COUSINS RUN AN AIRLINE! WE'RE GETTING GUESTS FROM ALL OVER!
CAMPGROUND TRANSYLVANIA
AND NOW THAT DRAC SCARED THEM INTO MAKING A DEAL, THEY'RE RUNNING THE PLACE, THE GREMLINS HAVE A STAKE IN HELPING IT SUCCEED!
STAKE? WHO SAID STAKE?
WHATEVER.
BUT, YOU KNOW, JOHNNY, I GOTTA SAY, THIS TIME, YOU DID OKAY!
WHEW! AFTER ALL THIS, WE COULD ALL USE A BREAK!
HMM.... MAYBE A CRUISE?
THE END

WATCH OUT FOR PAPERCUTZ™

CONGRATULATIONS! You've made it all the way through "Motel Transylvania" in one piece! Unless you're the kind of Papercutz fanatic that rushes to the Watch Out page first. Either way, welcome to the third terror-filled HOTEL TRANSYLVANIA graphic novel by "Spooky" Stefan Petrucha, our wicked writer, Allen "Ghostly" Gladfelter, our petrifying pencil artist, and Zazo "the Zombie," our insidious inker, from the House of Papercutz, those mindless minions dedicated to publishing great graphic novels for boys and ghouls of all ages. I'm Jim "Screaming" Salicrup, Editor-in-Chief and Dracula's Personal Tweeting Instructor, here once again to this time take you on a guided tour behind-the-scenes at palatial Papercutz headquarters…

Once you've stepped into our insidious inner sanctum, you'll be greeted by either Ishrath or Rebecca, intelligent young women who'll instantly make you feel right at home, unless you're a bill collector—in which case you'll find out why Ishrath wears a THRASHER sweat shirt!

Eventually (pay no attention to those skeletons seated in the reception area!) you'll be welcomed by Assistant Managing Editor Jeff "the Werewolf" Whitman, who, depending on the phases of the moon, will be either clean-shaven or excessively hirsute. He's probably in a good mood if he's just coming off a phone call with Virginia "the Vampire" King, but if he's just been tongue-lashed by yours truly, then be prepared to witness a display of various pouty faces. He'll probably lead you to his desk and proudly show off his awesome collection of Gumby figures. He may even read you some of the glowing reviews his stories in the GUMBY graphic novel garnered. Heck, he may even be wearing his official Gumby costume!

Be warned that Martin "The Madman" Zatryb, the antagonistic Art Director, may attack you (verbally) at any moment! We try to keep him sedated at all times by pumping the soothing sounds of such NPR hosts such as Terry "Gross" Gross into his ever-present headphones.

Suddenly, bursting out of his office, comes Papercutz publisher "Terrorfying" Terry Nantier, demanding to know if HOTEL TRANSYLVANIA #3 will be in stores in time for the premiere of the HOTEL TRANSYLVANIA 3: SUMMER VACATION motion picture. As he screams at me, I quietly reassure him that everything will be fine as soon as I finish writing the Watch Out for Papercutz page. Momentarily pacified, he returns to the soulful jazz sounds emanating from within his luxurious lair (otherwise known as his dimly-lit office). I continue my interrupted call, speaking to one of the greatest Papercutz fans of all, Rachel "The Beast" Boden, explaining to her that I need to speak, via The Watch Out for Papercutz page to all the rest of the Papercutz fans and conclude our virtual tour of our hideous hidden headquarters. Rachel's always very understanding and says to tell all the other Papercutz fans she says hello.

Little did I realize that, sitting at Arthur "the Fiend" Field's desk was none other than GUMBY artist Jolyon "the Shaved Yeti" Yates drawing the scene I just described featuring Terry, me, and Jeff. Here see for yourself:

Thus concludes our ten-minute terror-tour. I need to get back to work before Terry starts demanding to know how HOTEL TRANSYLVANIA #4 is coming along. We hope you enjoyed this somewhat-scary behind-the-scenes peek at Papercutz and return soon!

Fangs, er, I mean, Thanks, JM

STAY IN TOUCH!

EMAIL: salicrup@papercutz.com
WEB: papercutz.com
INSTAGRAM: @papercutzgn
TWITTER: @papercutzgn
FACEBOOK: PAPERCUTZGRAPHICNOVELS
FAN MAIL: Papercutz, 160 Broadway, Suite 700, East Wing, New York, NY 10038

COMING THIS FALL...

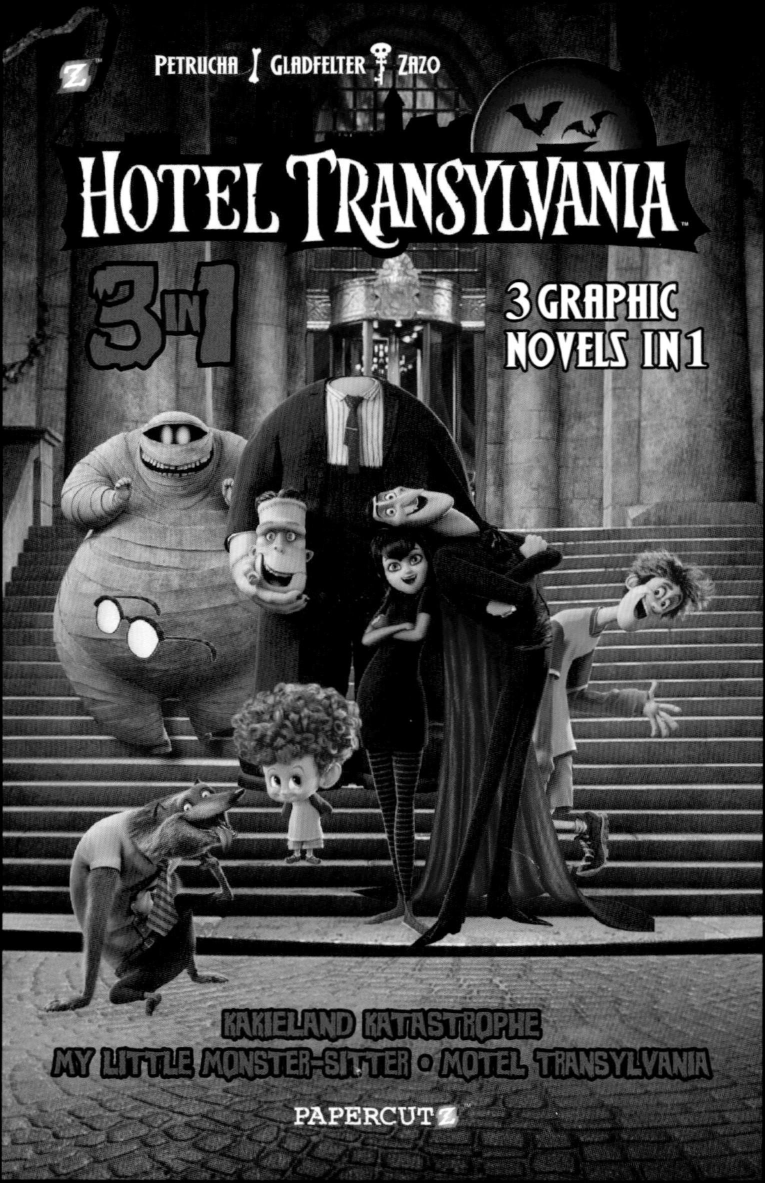
PETRUCHA GLADFELTER ZAZO
HOTEL TRANSYLVANIA
3 IN 1
3 GRAPHIC NOVELS IN 1
KAKIELAND KATASTROPHE
MY LITTLE MONSTER-SITTER • MOTEL TRANSYLVANIA
PAPERCUTZ

3 GRAPHIC NOVELS IN 1 CREEPY COLLECTION FEATURING DRAC, MAVIS, AND THEIR HOTELING HORDE OF MONSTERS!

papercutz.com

HOTEL
TRANSYLVANIA